MW01614188

# The Werewolf's Curse
## or
# Hair Today, Gone Tomorrow

**A Totally Outrageous
Supernatural Comedy**

by Billy St. John

A SAMUEL FRENCH ACTING EDITION

SAMUEL
FRENCH
FOUNDED 1830
New York Hollywood London Toronto
SAMUELFRENCH.COM

ISBN  978-0-573-62968-6     Printed  in  U.S.A.          #25650

### MUSIC USE NOTE

### IMPORTANT BILLING AND CREDIT
### REQUIREMENTS

# CAST OF CHARACTERS

## The Hero & Heroine

HARRY PATE—20's, handsome, American veterinary student
ETTA GREENLEAF—20's, pretty, American botany student

## The Villians

DR. FRANK EINSTEIN—30's or older, a mad scientist, British
PROFESSOR WONDER—30's or older, carnival owner, unscrupulous, American

## Professor Wonder's Carnival Troupe

BARON GUNDER BITERONDERNECK—200 years old, a vampire, drinks only fruit juice
HARRIET—20's or older, bearded lady
DIANNE NEEDLES—20's or older, tattooed lady, has only one
GREAT GIGANTICUS—20's or older, muscle man, puny
OPAL & PEARL JOINER—20's or older, Siamese twins joined at the fingertip. PEARL is nervous, OPAL more courageous
NICK GILLETTE—20's or older, sword swallower, has a chronic sore throat
MADAM CLARA VOYANT—50's or older, gypsy fortune teller
BELLA—20's or older, belly dancer, has a Brooklyn accent
QUEEN TOOTIEFRUITTEE—4000 year old mummy

## The Villagers

*(All the villagers have the last name "Doppelganger" and are played by the same actor. Their ages range from 20's to 70's.)*

OTTO—farmer
FREDRICK—butler
FREIDA—housekeeper
OLAF—village idiot
HEIDE—maid
BRUNHILDA—cook
HANS—constable

## The Monster

*(An off-stage voice; only an arm and hand are seen.)*

## The Mob

*(The carnival troupe doubles as the mob.)*

# SYNOPSIS OF SCENES

TIME: The 1930's.
PLACE: Dr. Einstein's castle in Rumania, and surrounding environs.

## ACT I

## ACT II

## ACT I

### Scene 1—A path in the forest. A stormy night.

*(The house lights lower and ominous music fades in. It plays several moments, then fades out as dark blue lights fade up on the forestage, below the main curtain. A few freestanding cutouts of trees are DR; DL is a stone doorway surrounding a heavy wooden door with a huge metal knocker, representing the entrance to Castle Einstein. During the scene, there will be dim flashes of lightning and the distant rumble of thunder, signifying an approaching storm. After a couple of flashes, HARRY PATE and ETTA GREENLEAF EN-TER DR, followed by DOPPEL/OTTO. <Herewith, the characters named "Doppelganger" will be signified as "Doppel".>)*

*(HARRY is a handsome American in his 20's, a college student who is majoring in veterinary science. He wears a trench coat over a suit and tie, and a fedora hat. He carries a suitcase. ETTA, his fiancee, is also in her 20's, pretty, and a college student majoring in botany. She wears a coat over a dress, and a cloche hat. She, also, carries a small suitcase. Their clothes and hairstyles reflect the 1930's, as will the other characters'. DOPPEL/OTTO is a local farmer. He wears work pants and shirt, boots, and a battered hat. He has a thick moustache that droops at the ends. He speaks with a Teutonic accent.)*

DOPPEL/OTTO. Der castle iss at der end of der path. You can't miss it.

ETTA. But a storm is fast approaching! Can't you take us the rest of the way in your wagon?

DOPPEL/OTTO. Sorry, miss. I von't go no closer to Castle Einstein dan dis. No von else in der village vill eeder, 'cept for der few villing to vork for der doctor. If you ask me, dey're touched in der noggin, efen if dey are mine own kin. You couldn't pay me enough to step foot in dot place.

HARRY. Why, may I ask?

DOPPEL/OTTO. Strange tings go on in dot castle, mister...very strange tings... *(Lightning and thunder.)* If you're determined to go, you'd best hurry. *(He turns to leave.)*

HARRY. Thanks for taking us this far, uh...

DOPPEL/OTTO. Otto...Otto Doppelganger.

HARRY. Herr Doppelganger...

ETTA. Yes, thank you. It would have been a dreadfully long walk from the train station.

DOPPEL/OTTO. *(Tipping his hat.)* Glad to oblige, miss; my farm's joost down der road. I do vish you two had a different destination, dough. If you bought return tickets on der train to vhere ever you came from, I hope you use dem soon.

*(He EXITS DR. Lightning and thunder. ETTA grabs HARRY's hand. DOPPEL will cross behind the main curtain and change costumes for FREDRICK.)*

ETTA. I'm frightened, Harry! What did Herr Doppelganger mean by "strange things"?

HARRY. I don't know, Etta. You can wait here for me if you like, but I have to meet this Dr. Einstein. He's the only one who might be able to rid me of...my curse...

*(Lightning and thunder.)*

ETTA. Yes...yes, you must... It is our only chance for happiness, darling. I can't let myself be a 'fraidy cat. I'll go with you... stand by you...support you...

HARRY. Oh, Etta...

*(He sets down his suitcase.)*

ETTA. Oh, Harry... *(She sets down her suitcase. They kiss.)* If only Dr. Einstein CAN help you...

HARRY. I fear he is my final hope. If he cannot find the cure...

ETTA. Hush! Cast aside your doubts! He can! I know he can! Why else would he have invited you here, after you had written him about your...condition...?

HARRY. You're right, darling. He must feel he can do something to remedy my affliction. If only I hadn't attempted to pet that wolf cub... If only it hadn't bit me... If only it had been an ordinary wolf, and not...

ETTA. *(Cutting in.)* But you did, and it did, and it wasn't! That can't be changed—what's passed has passed!

HARRY. What an astute observation. How wise you are. It is no wonder I fell in love with you at first sniff...I mean, sight!

ETTA. And I, you, too! *(They kiss again. Picking up her suitcase.)* Let us go meet this Dr. Frank Einstein and pray he can remove the dark shadow that has fallen upon us.

HARRY. *(Picking up his suitcase.)* Yes, onward to Castle Einstein! *(Lightning and thunder. They join hands and cross toward DL.)* Look yonder up the path, ahead.

ETTA. *(Stops; startled.)* A head!?!

HARRY. Ahead of us—there's the castle.

*(He extends his left arm, pointing off DL. Unconsciously, he raises his right foot slightly behind him like a dog pointing at game.)*

ETTA. *(Relieved.)* Oh...of course... *(They resume walking. Lightning and thunder.)* I see it now, silhouetted against the lightning. It looks so foreboding, like a great, gray, stone beast.

HARRY. Ha! Ha! What a vivid imagination you have, Etta, dear. What could there be inside Castle Einstein that could possibly harm us? *(They arrive at the door DL.)* We've arrived. I'll knock.

ETTA. Yes...

*(He bangs the knocker. The door is opened by DOPPEL/FREDRICK. He is your typical butler, dressed in a tuxedo. He is clean shaven. His manner is proper, almost to the point of being imperious. He speaks with a British accent.)*

DOPPEL/FREDRICK. May I help you?

ETTA. My goodness! You look like...

HARRY. You bear a striking resemblance to...uh...Herr Doppelganger—Otto Doppelganger—who gave us a ride from the train station.

DOPPEL/FREDRICK. Otto is my cousin. My name is Fredrick Doppelganger. I am the butler here. Our village is tiny and isolated; most of the villagers are related.

HARRY. But you speak English perfectly.

DOPPEL/FREDRICK. My mother was British, a rare outsider to these parts, who moved here when she married my father. I was taught to speak both English and Rumanian fluently. That is one of the reasons Dr. Einstein hired me—he, too, is British, you see. As I inquired before, may I help you?

HARRY. I'm Harry Pate and this is Etta Greenleaf. We're students at the University of Lipsync. Dr. Einstein is expecting us.

DOPPEL/FREDRICK. Ah, so. Please enter.

*(He steps back, opening the door. ETTA seems hesitant.)*

HARRY. Come, Etta. Hopefully, the solution to our problem lies within.

*(Lightning and thunder. They EXIT through the doorway. The lights fade out as the ominous music fades in and plays as the doorway and trees are struck.)*

**Scene 2—The study in Castle Einstein. Immediately following.**

*(The music fades out as the curtain opens and the lights fade up. The main set is the study at Castle Einstein. A narrow platform spans the US wall. At its SR end is an archway that leads to the laboratory; another archway at the SL end leads to the guest rooms. A set of French doors is UC on the platform, opening into the room. Beyond them is a veranda with a stone balustrade at its far edge. Stone urns with shrubs in them might sit on the veranda. A backdrop depicting a dense woods hangs US. A set of matching antique*

*chairs are on either side of the doors; old paintings hang above each. A narrow wall is at either end of the platform, with long walls extending DS from both. On the short walls are mounted animal heads or battle gear such as shields, swords, maces, etc. The long SR wall is a floor-to-ceiling bookcase filled with books. A large globe on a wooden stand is at its US end. In front of the bookcase, DR, is an old-fashioned wooden desk. There is a chair SR of it, and another one on the SL side. Centered in the long SL wall is a set of doors that open into the room. A pedestal with a vase of flowers is at its US end. A Victorian sofa is DL of the doorway; a matching chair is SR of it with a coffee table between the two. A round wooden table is DC with four chairs around it. This table and chairs will be moved US to the platform to make room for an insert set at times, and the desk, sofa and chairs might be moved to the sides, if needed, for the same purpose. If realistic furniture and set decorations can be used, fine, but if not, since "Werewolf's Curse" is a spoof, they can be faked. For example, the bookcase, books, globe, pedestal and flowers, and wall decorations can be painted onto the flats; the veranda balustrade can obviously be cut out of plywood and painted. In other words, for this play, you can't get too hokey, tacky or silly with the scenery.)*

*(After a beat, the doors DL open. FREDRICK ENTERS with HARRY and ETTA, who still carry their suitcases. Lightning flashes in the darkness beyond the French doors, followed by thunder.)*

DOPPEL/FREDRICK. This is Dr. Einstein's study. If you'll wait here, I'll go up to his laboratory and inform him you've arrived.

HARRY. Thank you, Fredrick. *(FREDRICK nods, then crosses to UR and EXITS through the archway. HARRY and ETTA set down their suitcases and look around the room.)* Dr. Einstein's castle is certainly impressive.

ETTA. Impressive, yes, but at the same time somewhat...over-whelming ... *(Lightning, thunder, then, suddenly, the sound of pouring rain.)* The storm has broken. We barely made it in time.

HARRY. Yes, we were fortunate. I pity any poor travelers who are out in the elements tonight.

ETTA. Indeed.

HARRY. Alas, it is not tonight's weather that concerns me so much as tomorrow's. It is predicted to be clear, and tomorrow night will mark the first rising of the next full moon.

ETTA. Oh, no...

HARRY. Yes... But, hopefully, with Dr. Einstein's help, I'll beable to resist going through...the change...

*(Lightning and thunder. DR. FRANK EINSTEIN ENTERS UR, followed by FREDRICK. EINSTEIN is 30's or older, a mad scientist, though he seems "normal" at the moment. He speaks with a British accent. He wears dark pants, a white shirt and white lab coat. We will become suspicious of his interest in ETTA, though she and HARRY won't notice it. Might he have some nefarious plans for her?)*

DOPPEL/FREDRICK. Dr. Einstein, Mr. Harry Pate and Miss Etta Greenleaf.

EINSTEIN. *(Crossing to them.)* Welcome to Castle Einstein. *(Shaking HARRY's hand.)* I hope I might be of help with your... problem...Mr. Pate.

HARRY. So do I, Dr. Einstein...and please, call me Harry. Thank you for seeing me.

ETTA. *(Shaking his hand.)* Yes, thank you, doctor.

EINSTEIN. You're both welcome. *(He takes her other hand in his as well and looks at them in a strange manner.)* What lovely hands you have, Miss Greenleaf...strong, yet delicate...

ETTA. *(Withdrawing them, self-conscious.)* What a nice thing to say...and, please, it's Etta.

EINSTEIN. Etta... What am I thinking? The both of you must be thoroughly chilled, and no doubt weary. Fredrick, take our guests' coats and luggage to their rooms, then have Freida bring in some hot coffee.

DOPPEL/FREDRICK. Yes, Dr. Einstein.

*(He will cross to HARRY and ETTA and help remove their coats.)*

HARRY. You don't have to put us up for the night, Dr. Einstein. Etta and I just wanted to introduce ourselves and let you know we had arrived before we registered at the local inn.

EINSTEIN. Nonsense. I wouldn't dream of letting you leave. *(Lightning and thunder.)* I have plenty of room, and, besides, I wouldn't turn a dog out on a night like this...or a wolf... *(More lightning and thunder.)* I think it's time we discussed the reason for your long journey here. *(Indicating the sofa.)* Won't you sit? The sofa is quite comfortable. *(HARRY and ETTA sit on the sofa. EINSTEIN sits on the chair SR of it. FREDRICK takes the coats and suitcases and EXITS UL. He will change costumes for FREIDA.)* Now...This...curse...you referred to in your letter... Start at the beginning and tell me all about it.

*(The storm effects will subside in intensity.)*

HARRY. The beginning... I am majoring in school in veterinary science. Last fall I transferred from my college in the states to the University of Lipsync to complete my studies. That's where I met Etta.

*(He takes her hand and squeezes it.)*

ETTA. I, too, had transferred to Lipsync from my school in America to earn my degree in botany. Harry and I fell in love, doctor, and had hoped to marry upon graduation, but now...

*(She takes a handkerchief from her dress pocket and dabs her nose.)*

EINSTEIN. Go on.

HARRY. About six weeks ago we had a break between semesters, so we planned a field trip, of sorts, Etta and I, to the Wacherstepinder Forest—Etta to collect leaf specimens from the vegetation there, I to observe any wildlife we might encounter. We were deep in the woods, miles from the nearest village, and we got lost. Night fell before we knew it. We had just got our bearings when, suddenly, we heard a whimpering sound, a sound obviously made by a creature in  distress. I went to investigate...

ETTA. Harry is very tender-hearted, Dr. Einstein. He relates wonderfully to poor, dumb animals.

HARRY. Thank you, Etta. As I was saying, I followed the whimpering sound and came upon a wolf cub whose leg was caught in a trap.

ETTA. It was a steel trap with horrible jagged teeth! The little cub seemed to be in terrible pain!

EINSTEIN. A trap set out by poachers, no doubt. Please continue.

HARRY. Well, I sprung the trap and set its leg free. I reached to pet it, comfort it, when the cub looked up at me with its strange yellow eyes, and then clamped its jaws down on my finger.

ETTA. It must have hurt awfully! Harry let out a terrific scream. They must have heard him in the village.

HARRY. It wasn't THAT loud...darling... I had a tetanus shot before coming to Europe, so I wasn't worried about that. I fear, however, that I was inflicted with a disease...a condition...whatever it is...that is much worse than tetanus or rabies or any normal infection... *(Great anguish appears on his face.)* Oh, Doctor Einstein, I fear I was bitten by...!

*(He stops abruptly and drops the anguished expression as DOPPEL/ FREIDA ENTERS DL, carrying a tray with a coffee pot, cups, saucers, creamer, sugar bowl and spoons. FREIDA is an old woman. She has white hair and wire rim glasses. She wears a black dress, black stockings and black old-lady shoes. She walks hunched over with shuffling steps that can take her quite a while to get where she's going. DOPPEL can get a lot of laughs with this character with the use of physical humor.)*

DOPPEL/FREIDA. *(With a Teutonic accent and a shaky old lady's voice.)* Fredrick said you vanted coffee, Herr Doctor.

EINSTEIN. That is correct, Freida. Place it on the coffee table.

DOPPEL/FREIDA. Ja, Herr Doctor...on der table...

*(She shuffles toward the coffee table.)*

EINSTEIN. Freida is my housekeeper. She is Fredrick's great-grandmother.

ETTA. How nice.

EINSTEIN. She should have retired years ago, but the old dear loves to work, so I let her continue. I just don't have the heart... *(He stops as if struck by a thought, then takes a pencil and paper from his lab coat pocket.)* Excuse me—I just remembered something I must add to my shopping list.

*(He jots down a word on the paper. Meanwhile, FREIDA stops.)*

> DOPPEL/FREIDA. Vhere am I goink?
> ETTA. To the coffee table.
> DOPPEL/FREIDA. Vhere iss it?
> ETTA. *(Indicating.)* Here.
> DOPPEL/FREIDA. Dere?
> ETTA. Yes, here.
> DOPPEL/FREIDA. Danke.

*(She shuffles on to the table. EINSTEIN returns the pencil and paper to his pocket.)*

> EINSTEIN. That's good, Freida. Just a couple more steps.
> DOPPEL/FREIDA. I vas hoping you vould zay dot.
> EINSTEIN. Now, set it down.
> DOPPEL/FREIDA. Vhere?
> EINSTEIN. Here.
> DOPPEL/FREIDA. Vhere?
> EINSTEIN. Here.
> DOPPEL/FREIDA. Here?
> EINSTEIN. There.
> DOPPEL/FREIDA. Danke.

*(She sets the tray down on the coffee table.)*

> EINSTEIN. You may go now, Freida.
> DOPPEL/FREIDA. Ja, Herr Doctor.

*(She nods, turns slowly, then starts her shuffle to the door DL.)*

ETTA. Shall I pour?
EINSTEIN. That would be nice.

*(ETTA will pour coffee into the three cups. FREIDA stops.)*

DOPPEL/FREIDA. Herr Doctor? Vhere am I goink?
EINSTEIN. Why don't you return to the kitchen and sit by the fire with cook?
DOPPEL/FREIDA. Vid der cook?
EINSTEIN. Yes, Freida, with the cook, your niece, Brunhilda.
DOPPEL/FREIDA. Vid mein niece?
EINSTEIN. Yes, your niece. Through the door and to your right.
DOPPEL/FREIDA. True der door...

*(She shuffles on to the door and EXITS. DOPPEL will change costumes for OLAF.)*

ETTA. What a sweet little old lady. *(Handing him a cup of coffee.)* Doctor Einstein?
EINSTEIN. Thank you.

*(He will add cream and sugar.)*

ETTA. You certainly employ a lot of Doppelgangers. *(Handing HARRY a cup of coffee.)* Darling?
EINSTEIN. I do what I can to help the economy of the village. Harry, you were saying...?
HARRY. Oh, yes. *(He sets down the cup.)* I was saying...*(He instantly resumes the anguished look and tone of voice.)*...I fear I was bitten by...a werewolf!

*(He buries his face in his hands. Lightning and thunder.)*

EINSTEIN. Most modern doctors and scientists would scoff at your claim, my boy, but I have no doubt that many creatures of mythology and folklore actually do exist, even today. *(He sets down his cup. His voice will grow in intensity.)* It is because of my belief in such beings that I was ostracized by my fellow practitioners, shunned by society, and driven from my homeland to this primitive country where I can conduct my experiments in peace!

HARRY. *(Lowering his hands.)* You were driven...

EINSTEIN. *(Rising abruptly.)* Yes! *(He will turn and begin to pace DR excitedly.)* My work is my life! And that is what my work is all about—life! In my laboratory I have created... *(He stops himself before blurting out the next word, and calms down.)* Well, perhaps I will show you later. But first, we must address your problem. You say you fear you have become a werewolf... After being bitten, did you transform into a beast at the rising of the next full moon?

HARRY. Kind of...

EINSTEIN. Kind of? What sort of answer is that?

HARRY. When next the full moon rose, I suddenly felt a strange sensation like...like...ants were crawling all over my head...

EINSTEIN. Go on.

HARRY. And then...there was hair...lots of hair...

EINSTEIN. Yes...

HARRY. And then...and then...I had this ravenous craving for a very rare roast beef sandwich!

*(He buries his face in his hands again, sobbing.)*

EINSTEIN. That's it? That doesn't sound so bad.

ETTA. But it is, doctor! You see, I am a dedicated vegetarian. The thought of eating meat repulses me. Harry was happy to convert to vegetarianism for me, but as long as this curse is on him, he can't control himself...not when...

HARRY. *(Looking up.)* Not when I transform. That first time, I ran out into the street, found a gast haus, and scarffed down three bratwursts, two knockwursts and a wienerschnitzel!

ETTA. *(Rising.)* I think I'm going to be ill!

*(She crosses US a few steps and stands, back to the audience, with her arms crossed at her waist.)*

HARRY. *(Rising.)* You see!?! You see, doctor!?! Etta and I will never find happiness together unless you can lift this curse!

EINSTEIN. Don't despair, young man. I feel I might be able to assist you.

ETTA. *(Turning back.)* Oh, how wonderful! *(She crosses back to HARRY.)* Isn't that good news, Harry? *(She touches his arm and they both sit back down on the sofa. To EINSTEIN.)* Do tell us what you have in mind.

EINSTEIN. *(Pacing again.)* I think we can assume that the reason you didn't transform completely into a wolfman is because the werewolf that bit you was just a cub.

ETTA. Yes, that makes sense. *(Handing Harry his cup.)* Here, drink this, darling. It'll calm you.

EINSTEIN. Do you exhibit any animalistic behavior when you're in your totally human form?

HARRY. None whatsoever, Dr. Einstein.

*(He begins to lap the coffee from his cup with his tongue, like a dog.)*

ETTA. Harry! *(HARRY stops abruptly and sets down his cup.)* What can we do, doctor!?! What can we do!?!

*(DOPPEL/OLAF ENTERS UR. OLAF is the village idiot. He has a thatch of Dutch boy style hair, a wild expression on his face, dirty old clothes and boots. He has a hump on his back, and he hobbles along, one shoulder held higher than theother, dragging one foot behind him. His tongue tends to loll out the corner of his mouth.)*

DOPPEL/OLAF. *(With a Teutonic accent, slurring his words.)* De're comink, mathter—de're comink! I thaw them from der tower! *(He hobbles down to EINSTEIN.)* De're in a caravan, like you thed, but dere vagon vheels are stuck in der mud! Oh... You haf guests, already... Beg pardon, mathter.

EINSTEIN. *(Sternly.)* Never mind that! Go to the caravan and lead Professor Wonder and his troupe here on foot—at once!

DOPPEL/OLAF. Yeth, mathter!

*(He starts to hobble US.)*

EINSTEIN. After that, I have another errand for you before you retire to your pig sty.
DOPPEL/OLAF. Yeth, mathter!

*(He hobbles to the French doors and EXITS.)*

HARRY. Who was that?
EINSTEIN. That was Olaf Doppelganger. He's the village idiot. I use him for errands now and then...simple ones...
ETTA. Poor thing. His home must be awful if it is like a pig sty.
EINSTEIN. His home IS a pig sty—I let him sleep in mine behind the castle. I raise my own pigs; I love fresh ham, bacon... *(ETTA looks nauseous.)* Sorry.
HARRY. But, doctor, how can you devote your attention to me if you have other guests?
EINSTEIN. It is because of you I invited Professor Wonder here.
ETTA. Professor Wonder?
EINSTEIN. He owns a traveling carnival troupe. It's pretty shoddy, to tell you the truth, but he does have one person in his employ who could well be the answer to your prayers.
ETTA. Who, pray tell!?!
EINSTEIN. A gypsy fortune teller. Her name is Madam Clara— Clara Voyant. No one knows curses like gypsies. She might be able to rid you of the one you bear.
ETTA. Oh, Harry! There is hope...!
HARRY. Yes! Hope!

*(He and ETTA rise.)*

ETTA. Dr. Einstein, how can we ever repay you? Though we haven't much money, I'd gladly give you an arm and a leg to make Harry well again!
EINSTEIN. I'll keep that in mind. *(Lightning and thunder. He crosses to the bell pull DL.)* I shall ring for a servant to show you

to your rooms. *(He pulls the cord.)* I trust that you will rest in peace.

*(The lights fade out and the curtain closes. Ominous music fades in and plays as STAGEHANDS set a few cutout trees DR and DL. During the following scene, STAGEHANDS will set up the laboratory insert set behind the main curtain.)*

**Scene 3—A path in the forest. Immediately following.**

*(The music fades out as dark blue lights fade up on the forestage. There will be dim flashes of lightning and soft thunder as if the storm is passing. OLAF ENTERS DL, motioning others to follow, as he hobbles to DR.)*

DOPPEL/OLAF. Dith vay...dith vay...

*(PROFESSOR WONDER and his TROUPE ENTER DL in single file behind OLAF. They are, in order of appearance:)*
*(PROFESSOR WONDER, 30's or older, is the carnival owner, a greedy, unscrupulous man. He has dark hair slicked down close to the skull, and has a pencil-thin moustache. He wears a loud print suit, maybe plaid, bow tie and a straw boater hat. He's a pushy American.)*
*(BARON GUNDER BITERONDERNEK, 200 years old, is a vampire who drinks only fruit juice. He wears a tuxedo and a black cape with red lining. He is from Transylvania.)*
*(HARRIET, 20's or older, is a bearded lady. She wears an everyday dress of the period, a hat and coat. She is American.)*
*(DIANNE NEEDLES, 20's or older, is the tattooed lady. For now, she has only one small tattoo on her arm. She wears a one-piece bathing suit type of outfit and a cloak. She is American.)*
*(GREAT GIGANTICUS <GIGAN>, 20's or older, is the muscle man. He wears a leotard and tights under a leopard skin tunic that crosses over one shoulder, like a caveman, and boots. He's kind of puny, a wimp. He is an American.)*

*(OPAL & PEARL JOINER, 20's or older, are Siamese twins joined at the tip of the forefinger <by using a flesh-colored bandaid strip>. They wear everyday dresses of the period, hats, and coats slung over their shoulders. They are American. They can be made to look identical, but they really don't have to be.)*

*(NICK GILLETTE, 20's or older, is a sword swallower who has a chronic sore throat. He wears black slacks, a colorful shirt with sleeves that blouse at the cuff, a sash for a belt, and a bolero jacket. He wears a sword in a scabbard. He is an American.)*

*(MADAM CLARA VOYANT, 50's or older, is a fortune teller. She has gray hair with a scarf over it, a peasant blouse and skirt, lots of beads and bracelets, and a shawl. She has a Teutonic accent.)*

*(BELLA, 20's or older, is a belly dancer. She wears a harem girl outfit and holds a large veil over her head. She has a Brooklyn accent and got her start at Coney Island.)*

*(QUEEN TOOTIEFRUITTEE <TOOTIE> is a 4000 year old mummy, but that doesn't stop her from being stylish. Wrapped head to toe in bandages, she, nonetheless, has eye shadow on the strips above her eyes and drawn-on eyebrows, red lipstick on the cloth around her mouth, a wig and a tiara, and an evening gown. She wears a cape and carries an umbrella. She's Egyptian.)*

HARRIET. You've got us in some pretty awful fixes in the past, Professor Wonder, but this is the worst! You know I hate to get my beard wet—it frizzes and I can't do a thing with it!

PROFESSOR. Oh, quit your complaining.

BARON. It's not the storm I'm worried about, Harriet—that's passing over. It's the sunrise that concerns me. One ray and—poof!—I turn to dust.

TOOTIE. Dust isn't so bad, as long as you stay dry...which isn't easy in this weather.

DIANNE. Watch out for that puddle. Maybe Giganticus should carry you.

GIGAN. I can't—I've got a bad back.

HARRIET. Wimp! Some strong man you are!

GIGAN. Oh, leave me alone!

NICK. I think my sore throat is getting worse.

OPAL. How long have you had that sore throat, Nick?

NICK. Three years.

PEARL. And how long have you been a sword swallower?

NICK. Three years. How long have you been Siamese twins?

*(OPAL and PEARL give each other an "I don't believe he said that" look.)*

BELLA. How long have you been a nitwit, Nick? Siamese twins are joined at birth.

NICK. I knew that! I just forgot. You don't have to get personal, Bella.

BELLA. Sorry, I'm not in a very good mood right now. I had a perfectly good job belly dancing at the Coney Island midway when the Professor said, "Join my troupe and see the world!" Well, all I see is a bunch of trees!

PROFESSOR. Stop your bellyaching. Dr. Einstein has promised to provide us a new attraction that will put our carnival on top again.

BELLA. Again? I must have slept through the first time. What about it, Madam Clara? Will a new attraction make us a hit?

CLARA. Ask me later—right now I got zuch a headache!

GIGAN. My feet are tired. Can we rest a minute?

PROFESSOR. No! *(Muttering.)* Idiot...

DOPPEL/OLAF. Yeth?

PROFESSOR. I wasn't talking to you! How much further is the castle? *(OLAF ignores him.)* Hey! How about an answer?

DOPPEL/OLAF. Oh, ver you talkink to me?

PROFESSOR. Yeah. How much further to the castle?

DOPPEL/OLAF. It's very clo-th. Dith vay...dith vay...

*(He EXITS DR. The others will follow him off. As they EXIT:)*

DIANNE. *(To GIGAN.)* I hope Professor Wonder is right about our becoming a big success. I'll never be able to buy any more tattoos if I don't start getting paid.

GIGAN. The one you have is very nice, Dianne.

PEARL. This place gives me the creeps.

OPAL. Just stay close to me, Pearl.

PEARL. Like I have a choice?

CLARA. I hope dis Dr. Einstein ve're goink to zee has zome aspirin. My head is killink me.

BELLA. You know, you'd think a good fortune teller would be able to see a headache coming and take something for it beforehand.

CLARA. Oh, zhut up before I put a hex on you!

BELLA. Touchy-touchy... *(To TOOTIE.)* Be careful what you say to Madam Clara, Tootiefruittee—she's crankier than the time she dropped her crystal ball on her toe.

TOOTIE. Tut-tut...

*(She EXITS DR, the last of the line. The stage is empty a beat, then OLAF ENTERS DR. He will lead the group back on in the same order, crossing from DR to DL where they will EXIT. DOPPEL will change costumes for FREDRICK.)*

DOPPEL/OLAF. Tho thory...dith vay...dith vay...

PROFESSOR. If you're the village idiot, I see how you got the job!

DOPPEL/OLAF. Tank you. Dere ver tree udder applicants, includink an imbezile. I vas zo happy dey picked me.

BARON. You mean we've been going the wrong way all this time? I knew I should have flown ahead on my own.

HARRIET. *(Griping.)* I was offered a job testing shaving cream, but, no, I had to join a carnival...

DIANNE. I sure hope this Dr. Einstein can help us. I've been on pins and needles to meet him.

GIGAN. *(To PEARL & OPAL.)* You know, girls, if this Einstein is a medical doctor, maybe he can perform an operation to separate you. Have you ever thought about that?

PEARL & OPAL. *(Together.)* What!?! And give up show business!?!

NICK. I hope he's a medical doctor...*(Rubbing his throat.)*...'cause I sure could use a prescription for lozenges.

CLARA. I just remembered someting... I should haf known duh fool vas leading us duh wrong vay; fen I read duh Tarot cards dis mornink, duh card vid duh castle tower on it came out—it vas upside down.

BELLA. NOW you remember... "Madam Clara sees all, remembers zilch..."

CLARA. You're goink to get zuch a hex...

TOOTIE. Stop it right now, girls! I won't have you fighting!

BELLA. Yes, mummy.

*(They are the last to EXIT. The lights fade out as ominous music fades it. It plays as the trees are struck.)*

### Scene 4—Dr. Einstein's laboratory. Shortly after.

*(The music fades out as the curtain opens part way and the lights come up on the insert set of the laboratory. The walls look like large blocks of stone. There are doors in the SR and SL walls; the one SR opens out and has a bolt; the one SL opens in and has an old-fashioned key in its lock. A barred window is high up on the UC wall. On the back side of the window is a curtain rod with a flat panel of black cloth hanging from it to mask the set beyond. There are strange-looking machines around the walls. As with the main set, they can be real, perhaps made from large cardboard packing crates, or can be painted onto the flats. They have gages and dials and knobs which can be turned, or actors can mime turning them. A real whip is coiled over a hook on the wall by the SR door. A folding screen sets in the UR corner. There is a rectangular lab table UC on which are scientific-looking items such as beakers, tubes, microscope, etc. You might even add some of the gadgets that can be bought in novelty stores which produce static electricity. A stool sets on the US side of the table, and one on the DS side. There is a gurney CS; on it is a sheet under which is a female dummy or mannequin parts. It is missing the hands, a leg, and the foot from the other leg. The audience will never see anything but its outline. You will proba-*

*bly want to construct the insert set by using a wide flat for the US wall with the side walls hinged at each end of it to open out, making it free-standing.)*
*(At rise EINSTEIN is puttering around the lab table, perhaps writing notes in a journal.)*

EINSTEIN. *(Talking to the body under the sheet.)* How fortuitous the Pate boy brought his fiancee. She's young and healthy and alive...so alive!...like you will be soon, my pet. Don't worry... *(He crosses to the US side of the gurney, lifts the sheet, and looks under it.)* I realize you still have one foot in the grave, my dear, but I'll have Olaf dig it up as soon as he gets back.

*(There is a LOUD BANGING on the door SR. His MONSTER will speak his lines off SR during the play, but will not appear except for one arm and hand, and—in this scene—a fake hand.)*

MONSTER. *(A guttural voice off SR.)* Mate!...Want mate!...Now!...
EINSTEIN. *(Lowering the sheet and crossing to the door.)* Good grief! Stop acting like a big baby! *(He unbolts the door and opens it; looking off SR.)* I know you want a mate now, but she isn't finished! You'll have to be patient—I'm doing the best I can! It's not like I can order parts from a Sears-Roebuck catalog!
MONSTER. *(Voice.)* Lonesome... Want her now! Now! Now! Now!
EINSTEIN. Calm down! There's no sense in losing your head over this! Leave me alone so I can get some work done!

*(He turns his back on the door and starts to pull it shut. The MONSTER's hand comes around the door facing, gripping it. The hand is green with black fingernails. Actually, it's a fake hand, rubber or a mannequin's.)*

MONSTER. *(Voice.)* Wait...

*(EINSTEIN slams the door shut on the hand without seeing it. The MONSTER lets out a roar.)*

EINSTEIN. *(Noticing the hand.)* Oh, good grief...

*(He opens the door a notch. The hand falls to the floor.)*

MONSTER. *(Voice.)* Hurts...!
EINSTEIN. Stop complaining! It could have been worse—go put some clothes on! *(He slams and bolts the door, then picks up the hand and crosses to the lab table.)* Patch...patch...patch... If he doesn't stop going to pieces every few minutes, I'll never get his mate finished! *(He tosses the hand onto the lab table.)* Now, where was I ...? *(There is a KNOCKING at the door SL.)* Hold on!

*(He crosses to the door, unlocks it, and opens it. FREDRICK ENTERS.)*

DOPPEL/FREDRICK. Dr. Einstein?
EINSTEIN. Yes? What is it, Fredrick?
DOPPEL/FREDRICK. Professor Wonder and his troupe have arrived. I showed them to your study. The Professor requested to see you at once.
EINSTEIN. Excellent. Show him up.
DOPPEL/FREDRICK. Yes, sir. *(He EXITS, closing the door. EINSTEIN pushes the gurney to the UR corner, then unfolds the screen to hide it. There is another KNOCKING on the door SL.)* Enter! *(The door opens and FREDRICK ESCORTS PROFESSOR INTO THE ROOM. EINSTEIN crosses to shake hands with him.)* Ah, Professor! Good to see you again. Fredrick, have Freida serve our new guests some coffee. (FREDRICK nods and turns to go.)* Fredrick? *(FREDRICK turns back to him.)* Our early arrivals...?
DOPPEL/FREDRICK. They are in their rooms. I believe they have retired for the night.
EINSTEIN. Good. Carry on.

*(FREDRICK nods and EXITS. He changes costumes for HEIDE.)*

PROFESSOR. Early arrivals? You have other guests?
EINSTEIN. Yes, Professor. *(Pacing SR.)* It was when I first heard from the American boy—a college student—that I summoned you here.

I believe he might be just what you need to turn your carnival into an even bigger success.

PROFESSOR. *(Crossing to him.)* That's what you said about Baron Biterondernek, a vampire who drinks only fruit juice! AND Queen Tootiefruittee! The way that woman insists on dressing and wearing makeup, she doesn't look like a mummy, she looks like a fashion model who has been in a terrible accident! The big draw at a carnival is always its Chamber of Horrors; the monsters you've supplied me so far wouldn't scare a nervous two year old!

EINSTEIN. None the less, they've made us lots of money, since we aren't splitting any of it with your troupe. My cut has been quite satisfactory.

PROFESSOR. I know, but I want more! I won't be happy until I'm filthy rich!

EINSTEIN. You're about to get your wish. Imagine the crowds you'll draw when you're able to show them—for a large admission fee, of course—a formerly pleasant, nice looking young man who, through no fault of his own, has become a hairy, snarling, blood-thirsty beast— a werewolf!

PROFESSOR. A werewolf!?! You mean the college student...?

EINSTEIN. Yes. Once I've finished with Harry Pate, he'll become a world-reknown attraction!

PROFESSOR. Once you've finished...? *(Suspicious.)* All right, Einstein, what's the catch?

EINSTEIN. *(Crossing to the table and sitting on the DS stool.)* Unfortunately, the werewolf that bit him was a cub. From the way he described his transformation, it's less a change than we require.

PROFESSOR. How do you propose to remedy that?

EINSTEIN. I'll instruct Olaf to set wolf traps in the forest tonight. Once he captures one, I intent to cut out the beast's pituitary gland and then graft it onto Harry's. After that, I'll pass a charge of high-voltage electricity through them. According to my research, that should turn him into a full-fledged, flesh-eating werewolf, and not just during a full moon, but permanently.

PROFESSOR. That's great! You're a genius! I can exhibit him day and night. I assume he has no idea what you have planned for him?

EINSTEIN. Of course not. I persuaded him that your gypsy fortune teller, Clara Voyant, might be able to remove his curse.

PROFESSOR. *(Crossing to him.)* Madam Clara? The woman couldn't remove a hangnail! The last guy she put a hex on discovered oil under his property the next day! As for seeing the future? She could stare at a calendar and not be able to tell you what day tomorrow is! It's a good thing we travel on to the next town before her customers realize that Madam Clara is just a big fake!

EINSTEIN. Harry won't realize that either. She'll keep him occupied until I'm ready to perform his surgery. The boy brought his fiancee with him, but I have plans for Miss Greenleaf—she won't be a problem.

PROFESSOR. Plans? What kind of plans?

EINSTEIN. Let's just say I intend to make a woman out of her—and not the way you're thinking.

PROFESSOR. I'm intrigued...

EINSTEIN. Don't bother to ask—it's a secret for now. I'll tell you this much—when my project is complete, I'll be able to offer you the most amazing pair of monsters the world has ever seen! But for now... I'm going to make you a snarling, snapping, totally ferocious werewolf!

PROFESSOR. I can hardly wait.

*(He begins to chuckle. EINSTEIN joins in. They proceed to loud, wicked laughter as the lights fade out and the curtain closes. Music fades in, a light tune, signifying morning, such as "Rites of Spring". A STAGEHAND sets in place a painting mounted on a stand so that when the stand is placed right behind the curtain, the picture will protrude through the split in the curtain, DC. During the following scene on the forestage, STAGEHANDS will strike the lab set and arrange the study set.)*

### Scene 5—A corridor. The next morning.

*(The closed main curtain represents a corridor in the castle. After a couple of beats, the music fades out and the lights come up on the forestage. HARRY and ETTA ENTER DR. They have changed*

*clothes to reflect that it's a new day. ETTA wears a different dress or skirt and blouse; HARRY slacks and a casual shirt, no tie. They will cross to DL.)*

HARRY. Did you sleep well, dearest?

ETTA. Very well, darling. Though my bedroom is large and dank and lonely, knowing you were just beyond the connecting door to yours gave me comfort. And you?

HARRY. I slept in fits and starts. I had such strange dreams... I dreamed I was in a forest. I kept running from tree to tree, sniffing them, and then I... Never mind.

ETTA. *(Stopping.)* Oh, Harry... *(They turn face to face. She takes his hands in hers.)* How I long for the day we can marry and I can sleep in your arms each night, to be there so I can comfort you when unpleasant dreams intrude upon your slumber.

HARRY. I long for it, too. Once we have breakfasted—on eggs and fruit and grain products, of course—I plan to seek out the gypsy woman who should have arrived with that Professor Wonder's troupe last night.

ETTA. If only she can help us!

HARRY. Yes... I fear the longer the curse is upon me, the stronger its hold may grow.

*(Unconscious of the fact, he lifts his DS foot and rubs it rapidly against his other leg, scratching. ETTA doesn't notice this either.)*

ETTA. Do you think it possible?

HARRY. I believe it might be.

ETTA. Oh, my poor Harry, baby... *(She takes his face in her hands and gives him a gentle kiss. During the kiss, HARRY wags his behind furiously. It stops when she breaks the kiss. She looks at him a beat, then says:)* Harry, you're drooling.

HARRY. Sorry! *(He takes a handkerchief from his pocket and dabs his mouth.)* Shall we continue to the dining room?

ETTA. That's a good idea...except I'm not sure how to get there. If I'm not mistaken, we've been down this corridor before.

HARRY. It does look familiar.

ETTA. That's the problem with these huge old castles—it's so easy to lose one's way. There are corridors and staircases and rooms everywhere.

HARRY. Again, you have made a remarkably observant observation! I suggest we continue to roam the hallways. With luck, we will eventually come upon... *(He stops when we hear the SOUND OF SOMEONE HUMMING a tune, off DL.)* Here comes a servant now...

*(DOPPEL/HEIDE, the maid, ENTERS DL. "She" wears a dirndl, white leggins and Mary Jane shoes. She also wears a blonde wig with pigtails, lipstick and rouge which gives her an apple-cheeked freshness. DOPPEL will speak in a falsetto voice with a Teutonic accent. She flicks a feather duster along the curtain.)*

DOPPEL/HEIDE. *(ENTERING DL.)* La...la...la... *(Startled.)* Oh! You nearly startled der strudel right out of me!

ETTA. We're sorry...

DOPPEL/HEIDE. Heide...Heide Doppelganger. I'm der maid here at Castle Einstein. *(She bobs a curtsey.)* Gut morgen.

ETTA. Gut...uh...good morning. I'm Etta Greenleaf and this is Harry Pate. We're Dr. Einstein's guests.

DOPPEL/HEIDE. I taught so. Dere are lots of strange people roaming around der castle dis mornink. *(Giggles.)* I vasn't referring to you, of course.

HARRY. I believe Professor Wonder's carnival troupe arrived last night as well.

DOPPEL/HEIDE. Dot vould explain it—der lady I saw vid a beard, I mean. Und der von wrapped in bandages. Und maybe der man sleeping under der bed who vouldn't let me open his curtains. Dot reminds me, he asked me to brink him a glass of orange juice. I had better fetch some from mein Aunt Brunhilda, der cook.

HARRY. If you're going downstairs, may we follow you? Etta and I were trying to find the dining room.

DOPPEL/HEIDE. Zertainly. Dis vay...dis vay...

*(She turns and crosses to DL where she EXITS. ETTA and HARRY follow. DOPPEL will change costumes for OLAF.)*

ETTA. Thank goodness! I'm famished.

HARRY. So am I. I'm so hungry I could eat a horse!...uh!...some borsch!

*(They EXIT. The lights fade out as light-hearted music fades in. It plays a few beats as the picture is struck. The next short scene will be played in total darkness. Since we hear, but don't see, the actors, it should be recorded and played on tape, or else DOPPEL will have to deliver HEIDE's lines from the wings as he changes costumes for OLAF.)*

### Scene 6—The Baron's bedroom. A little later.

*(The music fades out. In total darkness, there is a KNOCKING, then the SOUND OF A DOOR OPENING.)*

DOPPEL/HEIDE. Herr Baron...? It is I, Heide, der maid. I haf your orange juice. I eefen put two straws in der glass like you tolt me.

BARON. Ah, thank you. Place it on the floor at the foot of the bed, please.

DOPPEL/HEIDE. As you vish... *(The is the SOUND OF FOOT-STEPS, then a CRASH.)* Ach! Mein knee! Der dumkoff table!

BARON. Are you all right?

DOPPEL/HEIDE. Ja! Joost a little accident... If I could open der curtains...

BARON. No! No sunlight!

DOPPEL/HEIDE. Vell, if you insist. *(A FEW FOOTSTEPS, THEN THEY STOP.)* I vas vondering... You vork vid der carnival, but if you don't like sunshine, den how...

BARON. *(Cutting in.)* I don't do matinees.

DOPPEL/HEIDE. Oh. *(THE FOOTSTEPS CONTINUE.)* Der bed should be... here. *(THE FOOTSTEPS STOP.)* Der juice iss on der floor, vhere you vant it.

BARON. Thank you, Heide. Be sure you close the door completely as you leave.

DOPPEL/HEIDE. Ja, Herr Baron. *(FOOTSTEPS, then another CRASH. Strongly delivered gibberish:)* Gottenfurderheinnentableban-genhur-tenknee-in!
BARON. Heide...!?!
DOPPEL/HEIDE. Iss okay. I go now.

*(There is the SOUND OF A FOOTSTEP, FOOT-DRAG, STEP, DRAG, ETC. SOUND OF A DOOR OPENING AND CLOSING. After a couple of beats of silence, there is the SOUND OF JUICE BE-ING SLURPED. Then light-hearted music fades in and plays a few beats.)*

### Scene 7—Dr. Einstein's study. Shortly after.

*(The music fades out as the curtain opens and the lights fade up. It is a bright, sunny morning. The troupe is onstage. They have shed their outer garments and wear their show costumes. They are seated thusly: BELLA, SR of the desk; DIANNE, SL of the desk; NICK, SR of the table CS; CLARA, US of the table; GIGAN, SL of the table; HARRIET, chair SR of sofa; OPAL, PEARL, TOOTIE on sofa.)*

HARRIET. I feel wonderful this morning! It was great to have a real bed to sleep on, instead of a narrow cot like we have in our wagons.
PEARL. We agree! Opal and I have a huge double bed in our room. We've never slept so far apart!
OPAL. It was heaven! For once, I didn't have to put up with Pearl snoring right in my ear.
PEARL. *(To OPAL.)* And I had room to move when you tried to stick your cold feet against mine. *(To HARRIET.)* If we ever make enough money to retire and buy our own house, that's the first thing we're going to put in it...
OPAL. ...a huge double bed! Oh! Oh! Or better yet, we could buy a house with two bedrooms and put a bed on either side of the door-way that connects them!

PEARL. You mean we could each have our own bedroom!?! What a wonderful idea!

OPAL. It will happen, Pearl, you'll see. Remember what I've always told you—stick with me and we'll go places.

BELLA. When I retire, I'm going to eat anything I want and not care how big my stomach gets.

DIANNE. I'm going to open my own tattoo parlor—"Dianne Needles' Creations"!

TOOTIE. I want to fund an expedition to Egypt, find Ramses, and dig him up. He really knew how to show a girl a good time, if you know what I mean.

NICK. *(Sourly.)* Retirement? It's a nice dream, ladies, but at the rate we're going, we'll have to work till we drop. I can see myself fifty years from now, a doddering old coot who can barely swallow a butter knife.

GIGAN. In fifty years? Nick, you can barely swallow a butter knife now.

NICK. You're right, Giganticus. I'll never have a future with the carnival unless Dr. Einstein can cure my sore throat. Maybe Madam Clara can tell us what to expect. What do you think, Madam Clara? Will I ever be rich and famous and able to retire?

CLARA. Giff me your hand. *(NICK does; she looks at his palm and reacts startled.)* Och! You haf a tiny little lifeline! You von't liff annudder fifty years! *(Everyone reacts, concerned.)* You'll be lucky if you last annudder ten minutes!

*(Bigger reaction from everyone.)*

NICK. My lifeline...? Where...?

CLARA. *(Pointing.)* Dere!

NICK. That's not my lifeline—that's where I cut myself cleaning my sword.

CLARA. Oh, yes, I zee now. Dere's your lifeline. Not to vorry — it's fine. *(Everyone gives a sign of relief.)* Now, vhere vas I...?

NICK. *(Withdrawing his hand.)* That's okay, Madam Clara. I think I'll just let the future be a surprise.

CLARA. As you vish...

*(DOPPEL/OLAF ENTERS at the French doors UC, leaving them open. He has a burlap bag with mannequin parts inside slung over his shoulder.)*

DOPPEL/OLAF. Pardon...pardon...juth pathing through...

*(He starts toward the archway UR.)*

BELLA. That looks heavy, Olaf—maybe Giganticus can give you a hand.
DOPPEL/OLAF. I tink it vould be too big. Thankth, anyvay.
GIGAN. Besides, I pulled an arm muscle.
HARRIET. *(Sarcastic.)* Doing what? Shoveling all that food into your mouth at breakfast?

*(She coughs.)*

GIGAN. *(Sarcastic.)* What's the matter? Got a furball?
DOPPEL/OLAF. If you'll excuse-th me, I muth take tith to der mathter in hith laboratory.
DIANNE. So, what's in the bag, Olaf?
DOPPEL/OLAF. Oh, juth a few thingth he had me dig up.
DIANNE. This early in the morning?
DOPPEL/OLAF. Lath night.
TOOTIE. It sounds like you pulled a graveyard shift.
DOPPEL/OLAF. You could thay that.
PEARL. I'd be frightened, roaming about the village after dark.
OPAL. Don't be such a baby. *(To OLAF.)* Did you see anybody while you were out?
DOPPEL/OLAF. Theveral. I muth go or der mathter vill punish me.
BELLA. Punish you? How does he punish you?
DOPPEL/OLAF. He busts my hump.

*(He EXITS UR and changes for BRUNHILDA.)*

PEARL. My goodness, Dr. Einstein sounds very strict.

OPAL. You met him when he acquired you for Professor Wonder, Tootie. What do you think of the doctor?

TOOTIE. *(Rising and crossing around the DS end of the sofa to behind it.)* When they discovered me, near Cairo, Dr. Einstein had me shipped here to his castle in my sarcophagus. He brewed some tannin leaves to make a broth which restored me to life. The next thing I knew, I was part of the carnival troupe. You can ask the Baron what he thinks; I don't really have an opinion about Dr. Einstein since I barely got to meet him. *(Starting toward the French doors.)* I'm going out for a breath of fresh air. Anyone care to join me?

BELLA. *(Rising.)* I will.

DIANNE. *(Rising.)* Me, too. *(They start UC.)* You really like your fresh air, don't you, Tootie?

TOOTIE. You would, too, if you went four thousand years without any.

*(They EXIT UC and go out of sight UL.)*

NICK. I guess I should...

*(He stops as CLARA begins to twitch her head several times and moan. The others turn to watch her.)*

OPAL. Uh-oh... Here she goes again.

PEARL. I wish she wouldn't do that. It makes me nervous.

CLARA. I'm goink into a trance!

HARRIET. So what else is new?

*(Suddenly, CLARA collapses forward onto the table, her head making a loud BOINK!)*

GIGAN. Ouch! That had to hurt.

*(Just as suddenly, CLARA sits bolt upright, her eyes wide and staring. She will maintain the stare throughtout the trance.)*

CLARA. *(With a slow, eerie voice.)* I zee a young man...and a young voman...American...

HARRIET. She could be talking about us—most of us are American.

GIGAN. You don't have to worry about it, Harriet—she said "young".

HARRIET. *(Threateningly.)* Keep it up, Giganticus, and you'll be using your "great strength" to pick your teeth up off the floor.

CLARA. Danger...dey are in great danger... He iss in danger from der moon...

NICK. By "he" do you mean Giganticus or me?

CLARA. I don't tink so... Und der voman—she iss in danger of goink to pieces...

PEARL. *(Jumping up.)* She's talking about me! I just know she's talking about me! *(Excited, she runs around the sofa and above the table CS to SR. OPAL has no choice but to be dragged behind her.)* Oh, why did we ever come to this spooky old place in the middle of nowhere!?! There's no telling what is lurking out in those woods! If we don't leave soon, I know I'll go out of my mind!

OPAL. Stop it, Pearl!

*(OPAL brings their joined hands up and makes PEARL slap her own face with hers.)*

PEARL. Ow! You know I hate it when you do that.

CLARA. You are not der voman I mean...

PEARL. I'm not? What a relief...

CLARA. I haf not met dis voman yet, but I vill soon...soon...

*(She breaks the trance-like stare, flings her head around several times and moans, then flops across the table again, hitting her head with a BOINK!)*

NICK. She does that every time she goes into a trance. I'm surprised Madam Clara doesn't have a knot on her forehead as big as a grapefruit. *(Rising; to GIGAN.)* Let's lay her on the sofa.

GIGAN. Do we have to? I've had a touch of bursitis in my shoulder.

OPAL. For Pete's sake, Giganticus! You'll never get your strength back if you don't start getting some exercise.

GIGAN. Well... *(Reluctantly, he takes CLARA by the legs as NICK lifts her under her arms. They cross to the sofa and lay her on it, head US.)* I'm exhausted. I'm going to my room and lie down.

NICK. I'll walk up with you. I need to practice my act.

PEARL. Oh, good, Nick! With your sword?

NICK. No, with a tongue depressor. *(To GIGAN.)* Come on.

*(They cross to UL, GIGAN holding his shoulder, and EXIT through the archway.)*

OPAL. You never know if Madam Clara will be out for minutes or the rest of the day. Let's find the girls and see what they're doing.

PEARL. Okay, as long as we don't go too near the forest.

*(They start UC.)*

OPAL. I'll look out for you, Pearl. Don't I always?

PEARL. So far...

*(They EXIT UC and go out of sight UL. The stage is still a beat, then we hear:)*

HARRY. *(Off DL.)* Hello? Is anybody around?

ETTA. *(Off DL.)* We came down this hallway last night. I think Dr. Einstein's study is in there, Harry, beyond those double doors.

*(The double doors open. HARRY and ETTA ENTER. They don't see CLARA.)*

HARRY. You're right, Etta—it's the study...but where is the carnival troupe? Brunhilda said they'd be in here.

*(CLARA's eyes pop open. She lies still and listens.)*

ETTA. *(Crossing to the French doors; HARRY follows.)* The French doors are open... It's such a nice morning, maybe they went for a walk. That's something I'd like to do.

HARRY. Maybe later, Etta, but first I have to find the gypsy fortune teller and tell her my plight. If only she can rid me of the werewolf's curse before the moon rises full tonight!

*(CLARA makes a "so that's his problem" expression.)*

ETTA. I hope she can, too, with all my heart, but don't get too anxious, Harry. Even if she can help you, it might take some time.

*(CLARA, her hand at her chest, makes a "maybe, maybe not" gesture with it.)*

HARRY. If it does, I want you to lock me in my room tonight.

ETTA. I'll have Heide lock up both in.

HARRY. *(Gripping her shoulders.)* No! The transformation is... horrible! I don't want you to see me when...I'm like what I become!

ETTA. Harry, you're hurting me!

*(He quickly releases her.)*

HARRY. I'm sorry! Hurting you is the last thing I want to do! I'm just so afraid I might greet you in the morning with...bacon breath! *(ETTA brings a hand to her mouth, nauseous. CLARA frowns, confused.)* Let us try to find Dr. Einstein's laboratory. Maybe he knows where the gypsy woman is. Last night Fredrick sought him out there.

*(He gestures to the archway UR. He and ETTA start toward it. CLARA closes her eyes and groans. HARRY and ETTA stop and turn toward her.)*

ETTA. Look! On the sofa! Could that be she?

HARRY. It could be... *(CLARA moans, opens her eyes, and sits up groggily. HARRY and ETTA cross to her.)* Excuse me, madam... We are seeking a gypsy fortune teller who is here with a carnival troupe. What's his name...?

ETTA. Professor Wonder.

HARRY. Yes, thank you, dearest. *(To CLARA.)* Professor Wonder's troupe.

CLARA. I am der von you zeek. I vas expectink you.

HARRY. You were?

CLARA. Yes. I am Madam Clara Voyant.

ETTA. We didn't mean to disturb your nap.

CLARA. It vas not a nap—I vas in a trance.

ETTA. How exciting!

CLARA. Not really—dey giff me zuch a headache! But enough of my problems—it's your problem dot ve must be concerned vid, young man.

HARRY. You know...?

CLARA. *(Cutting in.)* I vouldn't be much of a fortune teller if I didn't.

HARRY. My name is...

CLARA. *(Cutting in; holding out a hand, palm out.)* Vait! *(She rises and will cross DR, pacing.)* Your name iss...don't tell me! Fuzzy!... no, dot's not right...Harry!

HARRY. Amazing!

CLARA. Und der young voman iss named...Edna!...No!...Etta!

ETTA. You're marvelous!

CLARA. Vell, if you got it, you got it. Unless I'm greatly mistaken ...und I'm zeldom mistaken...you, mein friend, bear der curse of der verevolf!

*(ETTA and HARRY are astonished.)*

HARRY. Did Dr. Einstein tell you...?

CLARA. *(Cutting in with a dismissive wave of her hand.)* Ach! Do not inzult me! I do not need to be tolt vhat I can zee for myzelf!

HARRY. My apologies, Madam Clara. You're right—I do have a malady.

CLARA. Hum it for me.

HARRY. Not melody—malady. I AM afflicted with the werewolf's curse. Can you cure me of this stigma?

CLARA. Ve vill zee... Zit! Zit!

ETTA. *(Worried; touching her face, feeling for a blemish.)* Oh, dear... It's the rich, Bavarian chocolate...

CLARA. Zit on der chair!

ETTA. *(Relieved.)* Oh...

*(She sits on the SR chair at the table CS. HARRY sits on the one SL of it. CLARA sits US of it.)*

HARRY. What must I do?

CLARA. First, giff me your hand. *(HARRY does. CLARA takes it and turns it palm up. Startled:)* Ah!

HARRY. What do you see!?! Is it the sign of the pentagram!?!

CLARA. No, it's grape jelly. Dot's really disgusting!

HARRY. Sorry. I looked around after breakfast, but I couldn't find a bathroom.

*(He hastily rubs the hand on his pants, then gives it back to her.)*

CLARA. Dot's better... Strange...I don't zee a pentagram, der true mark of der verevolf, but I zee a little triangle right dere.

*(All three lean in, faces inches from his hand.)*

ETTA. I see it, too. You're right.

CLARA. Of course, I'm right. You tink I don't know vhat I'm doink?

ETTA. No! You're wonderful! Madam Clara, the wolf that bit Harry was just a cub, so I wonder...

CLARA. *(Cutting in.)* I'm vay ahead of you. Yes, dot explains vhy der mark has only tree points instead of five. You haf der curse, but it's a pretty puny von.

HARRY. Does that mean you can rid me of it?

CLARA. Ve'll zee, ve'll zee...

*(EINSTEIN and PROFESSOR ENTER UR.)*

EINSTEIN. Ah, Harry...Etta... You're up, I see. *(He and PROFES-SOR cross to them at the table.)* Have you had breakfast?

HARRY. Yes, Dr. Einstein.

ETTA. We appreciate your hospitality.

EINSTEIN. You're very welcome. Am I correct in assuming this must be Madam Clara Voyant?

CLARA. Dot's very observant. Maybe you got a touch of der gift yourself.

EINSTEIN. From what Professor Wonder tells me, few have your abilities. *(Unnoticed by the others, PROFESSOR rolls his eyes.)* That reminds me... Harry...Etta...you haven't met the Professor. Professor Wonder, Harry Pate and Etta Greenleaf.

*(HARRY rises and shakes PROFESSOR's hand.)*

PROFESSOR. Nice to meet cha.

HARRY. Same here, Professor.

PROFESSOR. *(Nodding to ETTA.)* Miss Greenleaf...

ETTA. It's a pleasure.

EINSTEIN. I've informed the Professor of your...problem...Harry.

PROFESSOR. It's a real shame.

EINSTEIN. *(To PROFESSOR.)* Have you told Madam Clara?

CLARA. I know dis young man carries der sign of der beast!...vell, maybe not a beast, but zome kind of furry critter.

*(With a cry, HARRY buries his head in his hands.)*

ETTA. Oh, Harry... *(Gripping CLARA's arm.)* You must help him, Madam Clara!?! You must!

CLARA. I'll try. First tings first. I need to conzult der tea leafs.

EINSTEIN. I shall have a cup brought at once. Try to relax, Harry.

*(HARRY sits back down. EINSTEIN crosses to the doors DL where he will tug the bell pull. PROFESSOR crosses to the desk DR and sits on the edge of it.)*

ETTA. *(To CLARA.)* You can see how distraught he is.
CLARA. Ja, I can zee dot. *(She pats HARRY's head like you'd pet a dog.)* Easy, boy...easy...

*(HARRY lowers his hands and calms down. His sobs turn into dog pants.)*

PROFESSOR. Hey, Madam Clara, where's the rest of the gang?
CLARA. Zome vent for a valk. Der udders—I don't know. I vent into a trance.
PROFESSOR. *(Muttering under his breath.)* Trance—smance... The old broad's got narcolepsy.
EINSTEIN. *(Crossing back to above the table.)* I know Queen Tootiefruittee and Baron Biterondernek, of course, and I look forward to meeting the others.
ETTA. So do I.

*(There is a KNOCK on the doors DL, then the DS door opens part way. We will hear, but not see, FREDRICK.)*

DOPPEL/FREDRICK. *(Behind the door.)* You rang, Dr. Einstein?
EINSTEIN. Yes, Fredrick. Have Brunhilda brew a cup of tea. We need it at once. Freida is too slow—tell Brunhilda to bring it herself.
CLARA. Vid der leafs in der cup.
EINSTEIN. With the leaves in the cup.
DOPPEL/FREDRICK. Yes, sir. *(The door closes.)*
EINSTEIN. Brunhilda keeps a pot of hot water on the stove. It won't take her but a moment to make the tea.
CLARA. Goot.
ETTA. We were talking about your troupe, Professor. Who is in it?
PROFESSOR. There's Giganticus, the strongman...
CLARA. *(Muttering to herself.)* I'fe had cups of coffee dot ver stronger...
PROFESSOR. Dianne Needles, the tattooed lady...
CLARA. *(Muttering.)* Vid von little tattoo...
PROFESSOR. Harriet, the bearded lady...

CLARA. *(Muttering.)* Zomevon should take her to der vet for a goot groomink...

PROFESSOR. Nick Gillette, the sword swallower...

CLARA. *(Muttering.)* Who has trouble svallowink a drink of vater...

PROFESSOR. Bella, the belly dancer...

CLARA. *(Muttering.)* If she gets any bigger, you von't be able to zee der ruby in her tummy...

PROFESSOR. Pearl and Opal Joiner, the Siamese twins...

CLARA. *(Muttering.)* Whoeffer zed "Two heads are better dan von" never met doze two...

PROFESSOR. And as Dr. Einstein mentioned, there's Baron Biterondernek, a vampire, and Queen Tootie, a four thousand year old mummy.

ETTA. Goodness! A mummy and a...vampire!?!

CLARA. Don't vorry—he drinks only juice.

PROFESSOR. His father, a full-fleged vampire, mated with a Venezuelan fruit bat. The Baron takes after his mother.

ETTA. I'm glad to hear it.

PROFESSOR. Maybe you are, but my customers aren't too thrilled to pay money to see a vampire sink his fangs into a tangerine.

ETTA. Well, I think it sounds like a marvelous troupe! *(CLARA moves a hand in a "maybe, maybe not" gesture.)* Don't you think so, Harry?

HARRY. Uh...sure...

*(There is a KNOCK of the doors DL.)*

EINSTEIN. Enter.

*(The doors open and DOPPEL/BRUNHILDA ENTERS. BRUNHILDA, the cook, is in her 40's. She wears a peasant blouse and skirt, white stockings, and flats with a strap across the arch. She has a HUGE bosom. She has hair that is parted in the middle, then woven into braids on each side which are coiled and pinned to the sides of her head. Her pale pink lipstick and rouge should look like natural coloring, not make-up. She has a serious demeanor. She speaks with a Teutonic accent. She carries a cup of tea on a saucer.)*

EINSTEIN. Brunhilda—come in.
DOPPEL/BRUNHILDA. *(Stepping in.)* Fredrick zed you vanted a cup of tea.
EINSTEIN. Yes. It's for Madam Clara, here.

*(BRUNHILDA crosses to the table where she'll place the cup. Being top-heavy, when she moves, she tends to lead with her bosom.)*

DOPPEL/BRUNHILDA. Iss dere anyting else, Herr Doctor?
EINSTEIN. That's all. You may leave now, Brunhilda.
DOPPEL/BRUNHILDA. Ja, Herr Doctor.

*(She turns, flinging her bosom around first, and then crosses back to the doors DL and EXITS. DOPPEL changes costumes for OLAF. CLARA takes a sip of tea.)*

CLARA. Ahhhh.... Goot. I vas thirsty, anyvay. *(She downs the rest of the tea, chokes, sputters, then pinches a bit of tea leaf from her tongue.)* Dot's der trouble vhen you don't strain it. Now, let's zee...

*(She peers into the cup, as do HARRY and ETTA. EINSTEIN crosses to the chair SL of the desk and sits.)*

HARRY. Is there...is there hope?
CLARA. Don't rush me! You tink reading tea leaves iss like finding zee number in a telephone book!?! Giff me a minute. *(She swirls the leaves, peering at them. EINSTEIN and PROFESSOR give each other sly grins.)* Ah-ha! Goot news! I zee you cured of der curse! A potion vill do der trick.
ETTA. What a relief!
HARRY. How...?
CLARA. Herbs und charms...charms und herbs... I must take a little stroll in der forest to gather vhat I need. *(Rising.)* Dere's no time like der present. I vill go now.
HARRY. *(Rising.)* The potion... Can you make it for me to take before nightfall?

CLARA. How zhould I know! It depends on how easy der plants I need are to find. You vant me to start lookink, or not?

HARRY. Yes! Please!

CLARA. Den I vill zee you later. *(To the others.)* Later...

*(She crosses to the French doors UC and EXITS.)*

HARRY. *(Excited.)* Did you hear, Etta!?! Madam Clara is going to cure me! *(He runs excitedly to DL, prancing around with joy.)* I'll be well again! A normal human being! We can get married after all!

ETTA. *(Rising.)* Harry—heel! *(HARRY drops into a squat. ETTA crosses to him.)* It's great news, darling, but you must contain your excitement. Come, let's take that walk now; it will calm you down. *(She holds out her hand. HARRY licks it.)* Harry! *(He rises and takes her hand.)* If you'll excuse us, Dr. Einstein...Professor...

EINSTEIN. *(Rising.)* Of course.

ETTA. You are so kind to invite us here to meet Madam Clara, doctor. I give you my thanks with all my heart.

EINSTEIN. I accept both gladly. Go—have your walk. *(ETTA smiles at him and leads HARRY to the French doors UC. They EXIT and go off UR. Once they've gone, EINSTEIN crosses to CS.)* You're sure the gypsy won't actually come up with a cure...?

PROFESSOR. I'm positive. Every potion Madam Clara brews gives the same results—a ferocious case of the trots. The members of the troupe learned quick enough to avoid her concoctions at all costs.

EINSTEIN. Good. Then I won't worry about her...

*(He trails off as OLAF ENTERS at the French doors from off UL.)*

DOPPEL/OLAF. I got von, mathter! I got von!

*(He will hurriedly shuffle down to EINSTEIN.)*

EINSTEIN. You've got one what, Olaf?

DOPPEL/OLAF. A volf! I caught a volf in der trap, like you tolt me! Oh! Tho thorry... I didn't notice dot Profether Vonder vas here vid you.

EINSTEIN. That's all right, Olaf. You can speak plainly in front of the Professor.

DOPPEL/OLAF. *(Speaking plainly with no accent or slurring.)* So sorry... I didn't notice that Professor Wonder was here with you.

EINSTEIN. *(Smacking OLAF on the hump.)* Idiot!

DOPPEL/OLAF. Ow!

PROFESSOR. *(Rising and crossing to them.)* This animal you caught... Is it a fully-grown wolf?

DOPPEL/OLAF. Oh, yeth—it-th HUGE! It hath big, yellow eyth und long, sharp teeth. It-th a monthur!

EINSTEIN. Excellent. Bring it to the storeroom next to my laboratory, Olaf.

DOPPEL/OLAF. Yeth, mathter! Right avay, mathter!

*(He starts US.)*

EINSTEIN. Olaf!

*(OLAF stops and turns back.)*

DOPPEL/OLAF. Yeth, thur...?

EINSTEIN. Make sure no one sees you—no one else must know about the wolf.

DOPPEL/OLAF. Yeth, mathter...

*(He hurries to the French doors and EXITS, going off UR. He will change costumes for FREDRICK.)*

PROFESSOR. Now that you have a specimen, you can remove the wolf's pituitary gland and implant it in Harry Pate today.

EINSTEIN. No, Professor, not yet. The ideal time will be tonight, after he transforms and his own wolf-like manifestation is at its height.

PROFESSOR. Good thinking. I'll join you so I can see what my new main attraction is going to look like.

EINSTEIN. Till tonight, then, Professor!
PROFESSOR. Till tonight!

*(They begin to chuckle. It grows into a villainous laugh as the lights fade and the curtain closes. Ominous music fades in and plays as the tree units are set in place DL and DR. STAGEHANDS will place the insert set of the laboratory in place during the following scene.)*

### Scene 8—A path in the forest. Later that morning.

*(The music fades out as the lights come up brightly on the forestage. BELLA ENTERS DR followed by PEARL, OPAL, DIANNE, HARRIET and TOOTIE. They will cross to DC.)*

BELLA. No...no...not now...
DIANNE. Why not?
PEARL. You promised us you would one day...
OPAL. ...and this is the perfect day.
TOOTIE. We're usually either performing, packing, or traveling. When will we ever have another opportunity like this?
OPAL. We're here in the woods...
PEARL. *(To OPAL, not too happy about it.)* ...because you insisted ...
OPAL. ...where no one can see us.
DIANNE. Be a sport, Bella. Teach us how to belly dance!
BELLA. Oh, all right, I'll do it, but if I ever catch any of you trying to work it into your act...
DIANNE. We'd never do that!
TOOTIE. We're your friends, Bella!
BELLA. Well, okay... Watch me... *(The others spread in a line to her right.)* It's easier with music.
TOOTIE. No problem. *(She hums.)* Da-da-da...da...da... (Etc.)

*(BELLA begins to belly dance, undulating her stomach, swaying her hips, etc. The others join TOOTIE humming. BELLA is pretty good, and is featured a few moments. Then she says:)*

BELLA. You try it.

*(Still humming, the others imitate her. The result is comical. They don't notice HARRY and ETTA ENTER DL. The couple stops, surprised. HARRY stares at them a beat, then his jaw drops and his tongue lolls out.)*

ETTA. *(Noticing him.)* Harry!

*(She slaps a hand over his eyes. The others jump, startled, and stop dancing.)*

BELLA. Geeze! You nearly gave me a heart attack!
ETTA. I think you nearly had the same effect on Harry. *(She removes her hand from HARRY's eyes. His expression returns to normal. ETTA and he cross to the others.)* You must be the members of Professor Wonder's troupe. I'm Etta Greenleaf and this is my fiance, Harry Pate.
HARRY. It's a pleasure to meet you.
ETTA. That was obvious.
BELLA. I'm Bella, and I was just teaching the girls how to belly dance. This is Dianne, Harriet, Tootie, Pearl and Opal.

*(They ad-lib greetings.)*

HARRY. The Professor told us about you. We've already met Madam Clara.
ETTA. She read the tea leaves for Harry. She's a wonderful fortune teller.

*(The troupe exchange "yeah, right" looks.)*

DIANNE. Well, we're glad you think so.

*(NICK and GIGAN ENTER DL.)*

NICK. Hey, girls. We thought we'd join you.

*(They cross to the others.)*

GIGAN. I was going to take a nap, but Nick insisted.

TOOTIE. You're just in time to meet Harry and Etta, Dr. Einstein's other guests. *(To HARRY and ETTA.)* This is Nick, our sword swallower, and Giganticus, our strongman.

*(They shake hands and ad-lib greetings. GIGAN winces when HARRY shakes his hand.)*

ETTA. I guess we've met everyone except the Baron the Professor mentioned.

PEARL. Oh, we'll introduce him tonight.

OPAL. He stays in during the day.

HARRY. So Heide told us.

GIGAN. I don't know about the rest of you, but I've worked up an appetite.

HARRIET. But we just ate breakfast a couple of hours ago.

GIGAN. I'm a growing boy.

PEARL. I could use a snack.

OPAL. Now, Pearl, I've told you you're going to have to watch those snacks—I've been putting on weight.

PEARL. But Brunhilda's cooking is so much better than what we usually get on the road.

OPAL. You're right. Let's go see what she's planning for lunch. *(The troupe ad-libs agreement. They start DL. To HARRY and ETTA.)* Join us?

ETTA. We'll return shortly. You go ahead.

*(The troupe EXITS DL, ad-libbing about the food Brunhilda has fed them so far. ETTA takes HARRY's hand. They stroll DR.)*

HARRY. They seem very nice.

ETTA. Yes, they do. You seemed taken with Bella, especially.

HARRY. Now, Etta, don't be jealous. You know you're the only girl for me.

ETTA. You had better say that. If Bella gives belly dancing lessons, maybe I'll sign up for a few. Then I can dance like that for you. How would you like that, Harry?

HARRY. That would be great, but you'd better not give me a demonstration until after we're married. I probably couldn't stand it! *(ETTA stops, troubled.)* Etta, what's the matter?

ETTA. Harry, suppose we can't get married...? Suppose Madam Clara's potion doesn't work...?

HARRY. *(Taking her in his arms.)* It WILL work, Etta! It has to! If I couldn't marry you, I think I'd...die...

*(He kisses her. The lights fade out and somber music fades in. STAGE-HANDS strike the tree units.)*

### Scene 9—Dr. Einstein's laboratory. Shortly after nightfall.

*(The music fades out as the curtain opens part way and the lights fade up. The screen UR is folded out. The monster's hand has been struck from the table. EINSTEIN is US of his work table, filling a syringe from a bottle of colored liquid.)*

EINSTEIN. *(To himself.)* This sedative will knock out a horse, so it should be able to handle a semi-wolf.

*(The is a BANGING on the door SR.)*

MONSTER. *(Voice off SR.)* Want mate! Want mate!

EINSTEIN. I'm busy! *(He puts down the syringe.)* Look, I'll make a deal with you. *(Crossing to the door SR.)* Stand back from the door. *(He unbolts the door and opens it. Speaking to the unseen monster off-stage:)* Here's what I'll do—your mate isn't finished, but I need to get her out of my laboratory before the others arrive. I'll put her in there with you if you promise you'll just look at her, but not touch.

*(There is the SOUND OF THE MONSTER JUMPING UP AND DOWN AND CLAPPING HIS HANDS.)*

MONSTER. *(Voice.)* Promise! Promise!
EINSTEIN. Calm down!...and stop clapping your hands together! I thought I never would get the right one reattached!

*(The NOISES STOP.)*

MONSTER. *(Voice.)* Sorry. Bring mate! I'll be good!
EINSTEIN. You'd better. *(He crosses to the SL end of the gurney and pushes it to the door SR.)* There's something else you have to do. While my guests are in here, you have to be absolutely quiet. No one must see you until both you and your mate are ready to present to the world. Do you understand?
MONSTER. *(Voice.)* Understand...
EINSTEIN. I hope so—one peep out of you and the tongue goes.

*(He EXITS SR, pushing the gurney before him.)*

MONSTER. *(Voice.)* Mate! Thank you! Thank you! Big hug!
EINSTEIN. *(Strangled voice off SR.)* You're squeezing me too tight... Put me down!

*(There is the SOUND OF A PLOP! as EINSTEIN hits the floor.)*

MONSTER. *(Voice.)* Oooops...
EINSTEIN. *(Voice.)* Just get out of my way! *(He ENTERS, brushing himself off, grips the doorknob, and pulls the door part way shut.)* Remember—you can look, but don't touch! I'm warning you—if you break it, you'll pay for it! *(He shuts the door and bolts it. Muttering to himself as he crosses to CS.)* That probably wasn't a good idea.

*(There is a KNOCKING at the door SL.)*

EINSTEIN. Yes?

PROFESSOR. *(Off SL.)* It's me, Professor Wonder, and Madam Clara. Can we come in?

EINSTEIN. *(Crossing to the door.)* By all means... *(He unlocks and opens the door.)* Do join me.

*(PROFESSOR and CLARA ENTER.)*

CLARA. Zo dis iss vhere you'ff been cooped up all day?

EINSTEIN. Yes. I'm sorry I haven't been more hospitable, but there's always so much to do...

CLARA. You've got behind in your vork?

EINSTEIN. Among other things. Did you gather the items you need to make the potion?

CLARA. *(Patting her pockets.)* I haff dem right here.

PROFESSOR. It took Madam Clara a while, but she tracked them all down.

EINSTEIN. Good. *(He takes CLARA's elbow and leads her to the table.)* I believe you'll find everything you need here to brew it.

CLARA. Den I had better get busy. Night has fallen—der moon vill rise at any minute.

EINSTEIN. Indeed it will. I'll leave you to it. *(CLARA will go behind the table, light a candle or sterno under a beaker of colored water, take some twigs and leaves from her pockets, and begin to drop them into the beaker. Meanwhile, EINSTEIN crosses to PROFESSOR DL. They talk in lowered voices.)* I'm taking you at your word that the old bat can't really cure him.

PROFESSOR. Not a chance. What's the plan?

EINSTEIN. I instructed Fredrick to bring Pate and the girl here shortly. We'll let him drink Madam Clara's worthless potion, then when the moon rises, I'll sedate him after he transforms from a man into...whatever.

PROFESSOR. I can hardly wait.

*(There is a KNOCKING at the door SL.)*

EINSTEIN. Yes? *(He opens the door. FREDRICK is there with HARRY and ETTA.)* Ah, Fredrick... You've brought Harry and Etta...

DOPPEL/FREDRICK. As you instructed, Dr. Einstein.

EINSTEIN. Come in. *(HARRY and ETTA ENTER. To FREDRICK:)* Send Olaf to me. I might require his assistance later.

DOPPEL/FREDRICK. At once, doctor.

*(He EXITS and changes costumes for OLAF.)*

ETTA. *(Wandering around.)* My, what an interesting laboratory. What are all these machines? We don't have anything like them at the university lab.

EINSTEIN. I built them myself. I promise to give you a personal demonstration of how they work later, my dear.

HARRY. *(Nervous; crossing to CLARA.)* Are you making the potion, Madam Clara? I don't mean to rush you, but...

CLARA. *(Cutting in.)* I know! I know! I'm vorkink as fast as I can!

ETTA. *(At the door SR.)* What's in here? *(She unbolts it.)* May I have a look?

EINSTEIN. Don't open that door! I have some experiments in there which are extremely dangerous! I wouldn't want you to get hurt.

ETTA. Oh! How thoughtful of you.

CLARA. Zit! *(ETTA instinctively touches her face.)* Zit, Harry! Der potion iss ready! *(HARRY sits on the stool DS of the table. CLARA drops pieces of a broken Alka-Seltzer tablet into the beaker which makes the water foam. She crosses around the table and hands it to HARRY.)* Drink! Drink!

*(EINSTEIN and PROFESSOR exchange glances.)*

PROFESSOR. Drink it, young man. If anyone can break the curse, Madam Clara can!

*(He turns away and rolls his eyes.)*

ETTA. Drink it, Harry!

EINSTEIN. Drink it!

HARRY. Well... *(He brings the beaker to his lips and mimes taking a drink.)* It's bitter!

CLARA. You vere expectink lemonade?

ETTA. How do you feel? Do you think it worked?

HARRY. I...I don't know... *(He sets the beaker onto the table.)* My stomach is a little queasy, but...

EINSTEIN. We'll find out if it was successful soon enough. All we have to do is wait.

HARRY. *(Rising.)* If...if it looks as if I'm going to change, I want you to make Etta leave the room, Dr. Einstein. I don't want her to see me like that...

ETTA. Oh, Harry...

EINSTEIN. Whatever you say.

CLARA. You don't tink my potion vill break der curse!?! Dot's gratitude for you!

HARRY. Just in case...

CLARA. *(Putting her fingertips to her forehead.)* Ohhhh...ohhhh... ohhhh... I'm goink into a trance...

EINSTEIN. Does she do that often?

PROFESSOR. Like clockwork.

CLARA. I tink I had better lie down.

*(She crosses to the UL corner and sits on the floor. She moans and rotates her upper body a few times, then falls back on the floor, her arms splayed to the sides.)*

ETTA. Can we do anything for her?

PROFESSOR. Naw... The troupe is used to Clara sprawling all over the place. We just ignore her and when we move around, we try not to kick her in the head.

ETTA. Oh, I do hope her potion worked.

*(HARRY rises, a strange expression on his face. He moans and starts to scratch his head furiously with both hands.)*

HARRY. Itches...!

EINSTEIN. I believe we're about to find out.

*(A cardboard cutout full moon begins to rise beyond the window UC. It is attached to a fishing line and pulled up into sight by a STAGE-HAND behind the black masking cloth there.)*

ETTA. The moon is rising!
PROFESSOR. So it is.

*(He and EINSTEIN exchange sly looks. The moon will continue to rise until it's fully visible.)*

HARRY. It's happening again... *(His voice will grow raspier.)* The change... Get her out!

*(HARRY flings himself about, US, like someone in complete torment. ETTA watches, anguished.)*

ETTA. Can't you do something, Dr. Einstein!?!
EINSTEIN. I'm afraid not, my dear. Madam Clara's potion obviously didn't work.
PROFESSOR. *(Under his breath to EINSTEIN.)* Did I lie?

*(HARRY stumbles behind the screen UR making weird guttural noises. When out of sight, he will put on a fright wig of bushy hair that stands straight out from his head, and an equally bushy long beard. Meanwhile, EINSTEIN crosses to ETTA, still at the door SR.)*

EINSTEIN. You had better go, Etta. Harry doesn't want you to see...
ETTA. But I have to, doctor! I have to know the worst!

*(HARRY charges out from behind the screen, his upper body hunched over like an animal's. His voice is guttural, growling. ETTA shrieks.)*

HARRY. Meat! Want meat! Hamburger! Hot dog! Pork chop!

*(ETTA cries out after each meat is mentioned.)*

ETTA. It's horrible! Horrible!

PROFESSOR. *(Muttering to himself.)* But hardly a main attraction...

EINSTEIN. I was prepared for this contingency. *(Crossing to HARRY below the table.)* Harry! I have something for you! Look! *(He picks up a napkin-covered plate from the table and whips off the napkin. Beneath it is a pile of fried chicken legs.)* Fried chicken!

*(With a roar, HARRY grabs a drumstick in each hand and begins to eat them savagely. ETTA moans and buries her face in her hands. PROFESSOR crosses to EINSTEIN UC. They speak under their breath.)*

PROFESSOR. Ready?

EINSTEIN. Yes. I'll sedate him, then prepare him for surgery.

*(He crosses to the table, puts down the plate, and picks up the syringe. No one notices the door SR open behind ETTA. The MONSTER's hand and arm, in a black coat sleeve, extend into the room.)*

HARRY. *(Still devouring the chicken legs.)* Meat!

MONSTER. *(Voice.)* Mate...

*(He touches ETTA's DS shoulder. She lowers her hands from her face and looks slowly around till she sees the hand. She screams. She turns to face the doorway, sees the MONSTER offstage, and lets out a shriek that rivals Faye Ray's when she sees King Kong.)*

PROFESSOR. *(Seeing the MONSTER through the doorway.)* What in the world...!?!

EINSTEIN. The surprise I told you about—for your troupe.

PROFESSOR. I love it!

*(ETTA turns DS, about to run, when the MONSTER grabs her right arm.)*

MONSTER. *(Voice.)* Other woman no fun! Want to play with you!

ETTA. Over my dead body!

EINSTEIN. Well...

*(The MONSTER starts to pull her toward the doorway. ETTA screams, then:)*

ETTA. Harry!
HARRY. *(Engrossed in eating.)* Meat!
MONSTER. *(Voice.)* Mate!
EINSTEIN. *(To PROFESSOR.)* Get her away from him. We don't want him to bruise her lovely skin.

*(PROFESSOR goes to ETTA and takes her left arm. He and the MONSTER begin a tug-of-war with her. EINSTEIN puts the syringe behind his back and picks up a drumstick with the other hand, then crosses to HARRY.)*

EINSTEIN. Have another chicken leg, Harry.

*(HARRY slings the first two bones aside and grabs the new drumstick.)*

HARRY. Meat!
MONSTER. *(Voice.)* Mate!
ETTA. Help!
PROFESSOR. Let go, you monster!
EINSTEIN. This won't hurt a bit...

*(He brings out the syringe. OLAF ENTERS SL.)*

DOPPEL/OLAF. Fredrick thed you vanted to thee me, mathter.
EINSTEIN. Just because I sent for you doesn't mean I want to SEE you.
DOPPEL/OLAF. Vhat...?
EINSTEIN. Never mind. Give the professor a hand.
DOPPEL/OLAF. Vhere are dey?
EINSTEIN. Help him, idiot! Take the whip and make the monster let go of the girl!

DOPPEL/OLAF. Yeth, mathter. *(He hurries to SR and takes the whip off the hook on the wall. Muttering to himself as he goes:)* Vhy didn't you thay tho in der firth plathe?
EINSTEIN. This will relax you, Harry.

*(He brings the syringe to behind HARRY's head and mimes injecting him on the neck. HARRY stops eating and looks confused. OLAF cracks the whip.)*

DOPPEL/OLAF. Get back, you ugly brute!
PROFESSOR. *(Muttering to himself.)* Talk about the pot calling the kettle black...

*(With a roar, the MONSTER lets go of ETTA. She faints. PROFESSOR catches her and picks her up in his arms. OLAF EXITS SR, cracking the whip.)*

DOPPEL/OLAF. *(EXITING.)* Back...back...! *(The MONSTER gives mighty roars, then—after one whip crack—a meek:)* Ow...

*(HARRY starts to stagger about DS.)*

HARRY. *(Groggy.)* What...what did you...?

*(He puts the drumstick into his mouth, then falls to the floor. He passes out in a position that resembles a sleeping dog: lying on his back with his head facing SL, legs apart up in the air, knees bent, forearms up, hands limp, head lolled toward the audience with the drumstick in his mouth. OLAF ENTERS SR, closes the door, and bolts it.)*

DOPPEL/OLAF. It-th back in it-th room. Ith dere anytink else you vish me to do, mathter?
EINSTEIN. Yes, Olaf—take this syringe and sedate the wolf you trapped. Then you can assist me to prepare it and Harry Pate for surgery.

Before this night is over, Professor, your next attraction will be complete—a hairy, snarling beast of a man—a werewolf!

*(He starts to laugh. PROFESSOR joins in. Not sure why, OLAF joins in, too. All three laugh maniacally as the lights fade out. During intermission, STAGEHANDS will strike the lab and arrange the study.)*

**CURTAIN**

**INTERMISSION**

## ACT II

### Scene 1—A corridor. Later that night.

*(The house lights fade out after intermission; ominous music fades in and plays a few beats as a torch set in a wall bracket is put in place DC. It is mounted the same as the corridor picture is to protrude through the split in the main curtain. Once in place, the music fades out as the lights fade up dimly on a corridor. PROFESSOR and ETTA ENTER DR. He grips her by her upper arm.)*

ETTA. Let go of me, Professor Wonder! I have to get back to Harry! I must take him away from this horrible place!

PROFESSOR. He's not going anywhere, sugar, and neither are you—not until you're ready to join my carnival, anyway.

ETTA. Your carnival? I don't understand...

PROFESSOR. It's simple, my girl—at the moment, Dr. Einstein is preparing to perform an operation on your boy friend.

ETTA. To cure him?

PROFESSOR. Not hardly! When the doc is through with Pate, he won't be just a hungry, hairy college boy—he'll be a full-time were-wolf, the kind that eats people.

ETTA. *(Horrified.)* You can't be serious!

PROFESSOR. Sure I am. "Wolffie" is going to be a huge drawing card for Professor Wonder's Amazing Carnival.

ETTA. So that's what you're up to! I'll stop you! I'll tell the police! I'll tell them about you and Dr. Einstein and...and...that frightful creature he has locked up in his laboratory!

PROFESSOR. Don't kid yourself, kiddo. By the time Dr. Einstein gets finished with you, you and that "creature" will become very close.

ETTA. What do you mean?

PROFESSOR. Dr. Einstein made him from bodies Olaf dug up. He just told me all about it. The creature has a bride, but she's not all there.

ETTA. Who could blame her? Having to marry that monster would drive any woman insane!

PROFESSOR. No, doll, when I say "she's not all there", I mean she's ...not...all...there... That's where you come in.

ETTA. Oh, no! You don't mean...! You can't mean...!

PROFESSOR. I do and I can and Dr. Einstein will. He figures some fresh body parts are just what he needs to finish her up.

ETTA. But...that's murder!

PROFESSOR. Not really. You'll still be alive when he gets through with you...well, some of you will be.

ETTA. You fiend! How could you let him do that to me!?!

PROFESSOR. Now that you know about the monster, and what the doctor has planned for your boy friend, we can hardly let you go, can we? You'd do what you just threatened to do—run straight to the police. But once the operation is complete, you won't have a leg to stand on. Get it?

*(He laughs.)*

ETTA. You'll never get away with such a diabolical scheme!

PROFESSOR. Sure we will. Now, come on. Dr. Einstein wants you locked up in a nice, quiet little cell till he gets around to you.

ETTA. Help! Someone help me!

PROFESSOR. Yell all you want. These stone walls are a foot thick. No one will hear you.

*(We hear, but won't see, HEIDE off DL.)*

DOPPEL/HEIDE. *(Voice.)* Allo? Iss zomevon dere?

ETTA. Heide!

PROFESSOR. *(Startled; looking DL.)* Huh? *(ETTA stomps PRO-FESSOR's foot.)* Ow! *(She pulls free from him and RUNS OFF DR.)* Hey! Come here!

*(He runs to DR.)*

DOPPEL/HEIDE. *(Voice.)* Zorry, but I can't come dere—I've got vork to do. I'll go now und dust der dungeons.

PROFESSOR. *(Stopping; to himself.)* No wonder Dr. Einstein was so happy the Greenleaf girl showed up. If all he's had to work with so far are the local inbreds, his creatures are made from one big gene! *(To off DR.)* Hey! You can run, but you won't get away!

*(He RUNS OFF DR. Dramatic music fades in as the lights fade out. STAGEHANDS strike the wall bracket.)*

### Scene 2—Dr. Einstein's study. A few minutes later.

*(The music fades out as the curtain opens and the lights fade up. A duplicate of the moon we saw in the laboratory window now hangs against the backdrop beyond the French doors. The veranda is bathed in moonlight. A bowl of fresh fruit has been placed on the table. Inside the room are NICK, chair SR of the desk; GIGAN chair SL of desk; DIANNE, chair SR of table; CLARA, chair US of table; BELLA, chair SL of table; TOOTIE, chair SR of sofa; OPAL, PEARL, HARRIET on sofa. CLARA has a big scowl on her face.)*

BELLA. A werewolf, huh? He'll make a good addition to the troupe.

NICK. Yeah. If he joins up, at least he'll be able to make a living...and maybe we will, too, with him on board.

HARRIET. But Madam Clara said he doesn't want to be a werewolf.

TOOTIE. Well, we are what we are. Personally, I think being considered a monster beats lying around like a big dust ball any day.

DIANNE. Don't be upset, Madam Clara. I'm sure you tried your best.

CLARA. Der potion zhould haf vorked. Zometink must haf gone wrong.

OPAL. *(A whisper to PEARL.)* We've heard that one before.

GIGAN. The boy drank your potion, but transformed into a werewolf anyway?

CLARA. Dot's vhat dey tolt me. Right after I zaw him drink it, I vent into a trance.

*(A rubber bat attached to a line on a fishing pole flutters into view beyond the French doors.)*

PEARL. *(A whisper to OPAL.)* The way Madam Clara goes into trances, it's a good thing she didn't become a tightrope walker.
OPAL. Yeah.

*(The bat flutters into a French door with a BOINK!)*

BARON. *(Off SL of the door.)* Ow!

*(The bat flutters dizzily off UL of the door.)*

HARRIET. What was that?
DIANNE. I think the Baron's back from his nightly flight.

*(BARON ENTERS beyond the French door from off UL, one hand holding his nose. He opens the doors and enters the room.)*

BARON. I hurt my snout. I'll never get that flying business down pat. *(Crossing to CS.)* Where's Professor Wonder?
HARRIET. He went up to Dr. Einstein's laboratory hours ago. Why?
BARON. He needs to know it might be a good idea if we got out of here.
BELLA. Why, Baron? What's wrong?
BARON. When I flew over the village a few minutes ago, I saw a crowd gathered in the public square. They seemed upset about something—very hostile. Some were shaking axes and pitchforks.
OPAL. They can't be mad at us—we haven't performed for them.
PEARL. Yes...and Madam Clara hasn't told any fortunes.
CLARA. *(To her, covering one eye with a hand and glaring at her with the other.)* You vant me to put der evil eye on you!?!

PEARL. Sorry!

CLARA. *(Dropping the threat.)* Dot's better. Bezides, I couldn't zap you vidout getting Opal, too.

NICK. Could you tell what the crowd was angry about, Baron?

BARON. It was hard to understand—they were all shouting at once. I heard something about "strange cries from the castle" and "electrical flashes in the tower" and something about "vandals in the graveyard" and that Dr. Einstein's servant, Olaf, has been seen there in the dead of night.

BELLA. That's you, isn't it, Baron—"the dead of night"?

*(She giggles.)*

BARON. Don't make jokes, Bella—this is serious. I have a feeling we might all be safer away from here.

CLARA. Der Baron iss right—I am getting bad vibrations about dis place...

HARRIET. NOW you're getting them!?! Funny you didn't get any before Baron warned us.

CLARA. *(To her.)* I got a big hex I'ff been zavink just for you!

NICK. I wouldn't upset Madam Clara if I were you, Harriet.

GIGAN. Me, neither, Harriet—not by the hair on your chinny-chin chin.

CLARA. All of you, leaf me alone! I haf to figure out vhat went wrong vid der potion...

*(From this point, CLARA will withdraw into her thoughts and ignore the others.)*

PEARL. I think we should leave.

BELLA. I do, too, but Professor Wonder told us not to disturb him while he's with the doctor.

DIANNE. Then I guess we'll have to wait till he's finished.

BARON. Ah, fresh fruit! I'm going to have a little snack.

DIANNE. I asked Brunhilda to bring it in earlier. I know how you like something to drink after you've been out flapping your little wings off.

BARON. Thanks, Dianne. You're a pal.

*(He takes a pre-punctured orange from the fruit bowl, mimes piercing it with one fang, and crosses SR above the desk as he sucks the juice from it.)*

NICK. I've been wondering, Baron—have you ever tried drinking human blood?

BARON. Once. It was a fiasco. My father was very upset that I didn't take after him. On my eighteenth birthday he caught a milkmaid and brought her home. He tried to make me bite her neck. The best I could do was raise a little hickey. It was so embarrassing. After that, he disinherited me, and I've had to work all my death. That's why I hooked up with Professor Wonder—I have no money.

GIGAN. That hasn't changed—none of us do.

BARON. That's true, but being a part of the troupe has brought me something better than wealth. I'm finally with people who understand me and accept me as I am—I have friends.

TOOTIE. Amen to that.

ALL EXCEPT BARON AND CLARA. Amen to that.

*(DOPPEL/HANS ENTERS at the French doors. HANS is the local constable and wears a policeman's uniform including a helmet, a holstered gun at his waist, and boots. He has a moustache and goatee, and perhaps a monocle. He has an officious air about him and speaks with a Teutonic accent.)*

DOPPEL/HANS. Can I haf your attention, please!

*(The others react, surprised.)*

NICK. Who are you?

DOPPEL/HANS. *(Striding into the room.)* I am Hans Doppelganger, der local constable. I must zee Dr. Einstein at vonce!

OPAL. I'm not sure you can, constable.

PEARL. The butler told us the doctor locked himself in his laboratory and gave instructions he was not to be disturbed.

DOPPEL/HANS. *(Muttering to himself.)* I tink der doctor hass been disturbed for quite a vhile. *(Out loud.)* Der butler? You must mean mein cousin Fredrick. Vill zomeone zummon him for me, please?

HARRIET. I'll do it.

*(She rises, crosses to the bell pull by the double doors, and pulls it. She will return to her seat.)*

DOPPEL/HANS. (*Crossing to NICK, GIGAN and BARON SR; softly.*) Boy, dot voman has got zome five o'clock shadow!

NICK. Harriet is the bearded lady with our carnival. We're all members of Professor Wonder's traveling troupe.

DOPPEL/HANS. Traveling troupe, eh? Den you better pack up und get ready to hit der road. Dis castle is not a goot place to be right now.

TOOTIE. Why not, constable?

DOPPEL/HANS. *(Crossing to her.)* Vell, because der villagers... *(Noticing her bandages.)* Vow! Dot must haf been zome wreck you vere in! Vill der bandages come off zoon?

TOOTIE. Only if I get caught in a tornado.

*(There is a KNOCK at the double doors. The DS door is opened part way by a STAGEHAND who remains out of sight. HANS crosses behind the door. he will carry on a conversation with himself, alternating between HANS' and FREDRICK's voices.)*

DOPPEL/HANS. *(Crossing out of sight behind the door.)* Ah, Cousin Fredrick!

DOPPEL/FREDRICK. *(Voice.)* Cousin Hans. What brings you to Castle Einstein?

DOPPEL/HANS. *(Voice.)* I came to vorn you. Der villagers are revolting!

DOPPEL/FREDRICK. *(Voice.)* That has been my opinion of them for years.

DOPPEL/HANS. *(Voice.)* No, I mean dey really are revolting! Dey are advancink on der castle as ve speak, vid veapons and torches! I tried to stop dem, but dey von't listen to me!

DOPPEL/FREDRICK. *(Voice.)* By why, Cousin Hans...?

DOPPEL/HANS. *(Voice.)* *(Cutting in.)* Dey beleaf dot Dr. Einstein iss conductink unholy experiments in his laboratory. Dey fear him, und are determined to burn der castle to der ground!

*(The others, except CLARA, react to all this.)*

DOPPEL/FREDRICK. *(Voice.)* Good heavens!

DOPPEL/HANS. *(Voice.)* You had better vorn der doctor dot if he values his life, he had better leaf! I haf already varned his guests ...*(HANS' arm appears from behind the door as he gestures at the troupe, then is pulled back.)*...zo if dey haf good zense, dey vill go far from here as qvickly as possible!

DOPPEL/FREDRICK. *(Voice.)* I shall send Olaf to inform the doctor, and I'll tell the other servants. I'll make sure our relatives get out safely. Thank you, Hans.

DOPPEL/HANS. *(Voice.)* You're velcome. Didn't I vorn you all not to vork for dot man!?! Didn't I tell you...!?!

DOPPEL/FREDRICK. *(Voice.)* *(Cutting in.)* We can discuss it at the next reunion. Now I must...

DOPPEL/HANS. *(Voice.)* *(Cutting in.)* Yes! Go! Tell der udders! Hurry! *(HANS crosses into the room from behind the door. The STAGE-HAND closes it.)* You heard, no doubt?

DIANNE. *(Rising.)* Yes... We want to thank you, too, for the warning, constable. *(The others, except CLARA, rise, ad-libbing thanks.)* We'll leave immediately.

CLARA. *(Muttering to herself.)* I put in von pinch of sassafras bark...

DOPPEL/HANS. I vill try to delay der mob, but I am afraid dey are beyond control. Goot luck!

*(He EXITS through the French doors.)*

BARON. You see? I knew those villagers weren't organizing a bake sale.

PEARL. I said we should never have come here! I told you I didn't like this place, didn't I, Opal!?! Didn't I!?!

OPAL. Incessantly. Now, calm down, Pearl, before you hyperventilate and we both faint.

*(The cast members offstage and the tech crew begin to MUMBLE SOFTLY in the distance off UL and UR.)*

TOOTIE. Listen!
CLARA. *(Muttering.)* ...crushed caravay zeeds...
BELLA. The villagers!

*(All but CLARA run to the veranda and look down over the railing, backs to the audience.)*

CLARA. *(Muttering.)* ...zome rutabaga root...
NICK. Look! They're coming up the foot of the hill!
CLARA. *(Muttering.)* ...zome chili pepper to giff it zome zip...
GIGAN. They're getting closer!

*(Everyone onstage except CLARA, backs still to audience, adds a SOFT MUMBLE to the other sound to make the mob seem closer. Such silliness should get a laugh.)*

CLARA. *(Muttering.)* ...a bay leaf...
HARRIET. We have to get out of here!
ETTA. *(Off UR.)* Help! Somebody help me!

*(Everyone on the veranda wheels around, facing the room.)*

CLARA. *(Muttering.)* ...a tiny little beetle, but dot vas an  accident...
ETTA. *(RUNNING ON UR, distraught.)* Please, help me!

*(Everyone on the veranda rushes into the room, spreading US of ETTA who is CS.)*

BELLA. Etta, what's wrong!?!
TOOTIE. Why are you so wound up?

OPAL. *(To PEARL.)* That sounds strange, coming from her.

ETTA. *(Catching her breath.)* Don't let him take me!

NICK. Who?

ETTA. Professor Wonder!

NICK. Professor Wonder?

CLARA. *(Muttering.)*...zome crab grass...

NICK. Why are you running from Professor Wonder?

ETTA. He's a terrible man! He and Dr. Einstein have concocted a horrible scheme! They plan to turn Harry into a real werewolf—permanently! The man I love would be gone forever!

THE OTHERS EXCEPT CLARA. No!

ETTA. Yes! That's not all! Dr. Einstein has created a monster from dead bodies, and is making it a mate. Whatever parts he's missing, he plans to take from ME!

THE OTHERS EXCEPT CLARA. No!

ETTA. Yes!

BELLA. You poor girl... No wonder you're so torn up!

CLARA. *(Muttering.)* ...pine needles...

HARRIET. Why would the Professor condone such evil deeds?

ETTA. Because he wants to display the monster, his bride, and Harry in your carnival.

TOOTIE. That just won't do! Baron and I were already among the undead when Dr. Einstein found us, but to kill someone...!

BARON. And to turn a semi-lycanthrope into a full-time werewolf... No! We won't let them get away with it! *(To ETTA.)* I don't believe we've met. Baron Biterondernek...

ETTA. Etta Greenleaf.

*(They shake hands.)*

CLARA. *(Muttering.)* ...parsley, sage, rosemary and thyme...

PROFESSOR. *(RUNNING IN UR.)* There you are! Come with me! *(He takes a step toward ETTA, but the others except CLARA move to surround her.)* Hey! Move out of the way, you guys! Dr. Einstein needs the girl.

BELLA. We heard—and Etta told us what he needs her for!

PROFESSOR. So? Think of what it'll do for business.

DIANNE. We don't need that kind of business, Professor.

*(The others except CLARA ad-lib agreement.)*

PROFESSOR. I don't have time to argue with you.

GIGAN. You got that right—there's an angry mob on the way here to burn the castle to the ground.

PROFESSOR. What!?! Then we've got to hurry! She's coming with me! Get out of the way!

*(The group tightens around ETTA even more protectively.)*

GIGAN. You're not taking Etta anywhere, Professor.

*(He brings up his fists and strikes a pretty pathetic-looking boxing stance.)*

PROFESSOR. Oh, yeah? Who's going to stop me? You? *(He laughs.)* That's a laugh.

NICK. *(Drawing his sword from its scabbard.)* I'll stop you!

*(The others, except CLARA, ad-lib "And I!", "Me, too!", etc. PRO-FESSOR takes a step backward.)*

CLARA. *(Muttering.)*...a four-leaf clover...

PROFESSOR. I'm warning you—you had better do what I tell you or I'll fire you!

TOOTIE. Don't bother—I quit!

OPAL. So do I! Pearl can stay on if she wants to.

PEARL. Never, sister!—not now that I know what a mean man Professor Wonder is!

*(The others except CLARA ad-lib forcefully that they quit as well. The offstage MUMBLE grows louder.)*

HARRIET. The villagers are almost here! We have to escape while we can!

ETTA. I won't go without Harry!

NICK. Don't worry, Etta! Professor Wonder is going to take us to him...(*To PROFESSOR, brandishing the sword.*)...now!

PROFESSOR. (*Nervous.*) Uh...this way...

(*He hurries to UR. The others, except BARON, BELLA and CLARA, follow.*)

BARON. I'll fly out and check on the mob!

(*He runs through the French doors, spreads his cape, and jumps out of sight off UL, EXITING. A moment later, the bat flutters by outside.*)

CLARA. (*Muttering.*) ...castor oil...

(*BELLA runs to CLARA, grabs her hand, snapping her reverie, and pulls her to her feet.*)

BELLA. Come on, Clara! Hurry!

(*She pulls CLARA UR.*)

CLARA. Are vee goink zomevhere...?

(*They EXIT. Frenzied music fades in as the lights fade out and the curtain closes. The members of the troupe quickly throw peasant disguises over their costumes—old, worn coats, capes, shawls, scarves, mufflers, blankets, hats, etc., and grab axes, pitchforks and torches with fake fire. They're going to double immediately as the angry mob. Each actor will disguise his or her voice and speak with a Teutonic accent. If any of the tech crew are available, they can join the mob as well. STAGE-HANDS set the cutout trees DL and DR on the forestage. During the next scene, they will put the laboratory set in place behind the curtain.*)

### Scene 3—A path in the forest. Immediately following.

*(The music fades out as lights fade up dimly on the forestage, suggesting moonlight. The mob ad-libs angrily off DR. HANS RUSHES IN DL. The mob ENTERS DR. They will meet DC. The lines are designated by the carnival troupe characters' names, but the actors will speak as the characters they are doubling.)*

DOPPEL/HANS. Stop! Don't go any furzer!

BELLA. Get out of our vay, Cousin Hans!

DIANNE. Ja! Ve haf to do vhat ve haf to do!

BARON. Dot place is evil—evil! It must be destroyed!

TOOTIE. Ve don't vant to hurt you, brudder-in-law, but you can't stop us!

DOPPEL/HANS. I'fe tolt our relatives to get out, but dere are udder people in der castle—innozent people!

PEARL. Dey'll haf to fend for demselves!

HARRIET. Vhen dey associate vid Dr. Einstein, dey do zo at dere own risk!

DOPPEL/HANS. Von't any of you listen to reason!?! Vhere is Uncle Otto?

NICK. Oh, he hass a cold—he couldn't make it.

DOPPEL/HANS. Please, tink vhat you're doink! Tink!

OPAL. Never! On to der castle!

*(The mob takes a step, in unison, toward HANS.)*

DOPPEL/HANS. Vait! *(The mob stops in unison.)* I haf an idea—I could zite der doctor for disturbing der peace und threaten to fine him iff he doesn't cut it out.

GIGAN. It's too late for dot! Der time to act is now!

*(The mob ad-libs agreement.)*

CLARA. My great-nephew twice removed iss right! Ve must attack der castle now!

MOB. Attack! Attack! Attack!

*(The mob ad-libs angrily as they surge to DL. As they pass HANS, GI-GAN and BARON grab his legs and lift him up in the air so that he is bourn off DL in the middle of the crowd, still facing SR.)*

DOPPEL/HANS. Vait! Stop! Put me down or you'll be zoooor-rrryyyy...

*(All EXIT DL as the lights fade out and frenzied music fades in. The troupe throws off their villager disguises. HANS changes costumes for OLAF. STAGEHANDS strike the trees.)*

**Scene 4—Dr. Einstein's laboratory. Immediately following.**

*(The music fades out as the curtain opens and the lights fade up on the laboratory. The moon still hangs beyond the window. The door SR is bolted; the one SL is locked. The beaker with Clara's potion is still on the table. The gurney is back CS; the sheet and mannequin parts have been struck. HARRY lies on it on his stomach, face toward the audience. He seems to be bound by ropes at the wrists and ankles which pass through large eye-screws set in the four corners of the gurney. The ropes are not really tied, and later HARRY will be able to pull them free easily. He still has a bushy beard and hair, and he speaks with a raspy voice. EINSTEIN rushes among the machines, flipping switches and turning dials. Novelty electrical devices, if used, flash static electricity, etc. From this point on, the "mad scientist" part of his nature is dominant.)*

HARRY. Why have you bound me to this gurney, Dr. Einstein!?! I won't harm you! Set me free!
EINSTEIN. Oh, I'm not worried that you'll hurt me; I know you don't eat human flesh—yet!
HARRY. Yet? What do you mean "yet"!?!
EINSTEIN. In just a few moments, I am going to perform a little surgery on you, Harry. First, I must charge my machines up to full power.

*(He continues with the dials and switches.)*

HARRY. Surgery!?! What kind of surgery!?!

EINSTEIN. *(He picks up a vial of water with a pearl onion inside from the table and carries it to DS of the gurney; showing it to HARRY.)* A pituitary gland implant—a procedure I devised myself. See this, Harry? It's the pituitary gland I removed from a wolf earlier tonight. I am going to graft it onto your own pituitary gland, activate both with a super-charge of electricity, and transform you into a proper, man-eating werewolf, not some weenie-muncher who needs a shave and a haircut.

HARRY. You're insane!

EINSTEIN. Sticks and stones... *(He moves back to the table and replaces the vial.)* Sorry, but I'm fresh out of anesthetic. I'm afraid this is going to hurt a bit. *(He picks up a scalpel.)* I'll work as quickly as I can.

*(There is a BANGING on the door SR.)*

MONSTER. *(Voice, off SR.)* Mate! I want mate!

HARRY. What is that!?!

EINSTEIN. *(Putting down the scalpel; exasperated.)* I don't know why he won't go to sleep—it's way past his bedtime...and I gave him his foo-foo. *(Crossing to the door SR.)* To answer your question, it's a man, but he's only a few weeks old. I made him myself.

HARRY. You made him!?! But...that's not natural!

EINSTEIN. You should talk, fuzz-face.

MONSTER. *(Voice.) (BANGING.)* Want mate now! You promised!

EINSTEIN. *(Unbolting the door.)* Don't get your knickers in a twist! They're very hard to come by in your size. *(He opens the door.)* Look! How many times have I told you to be patient?

MONSTER. *(Voice.)* Don't know...can only count to three...

EINSTEIN. It's more like three hundred! I'll finish your mate as soon as I can, but first I have a delicate operation to perform, so I need quiet.

HARRY. I can wait.

MONSTER. *(Voice.)* Make mate first! Make mate first!

EINSTEIN. No! Making your mate at this point is going to be like starting from scratch, thanks to you! I told you you could look at her, but not touch! See what you did!?!

MONSTER. *(Voice.)* Sorry... Was playing hide and seek. Found most of her...

EINSTEIN. Well, find the rest...and be quiet about it ! Then we'll talk! *(He slams and bolts the door.) (To himself:)* I'll be glad when the Professor takes him off my hands.

HARRY. Professor? Professor Wonder? You're giving that... thing...to him?

EINSTEIN. Selling, my boy, selling for a hefty price, plus a percentage of his future profits. I have the same deal set for you.

HARRY. The Professor can't afford to buy us. His troupe says his carnival is barely scraping by.

EINSTEIN. Don't kid yourself. Wonder is making a ton of money, he just cries poor to keep his employees fooled. I probably shouldn't have told you that, but you won't be able to let the cat out of the bag. An hour from now, the most you'll be able to do is growl, not talk, and the only thing you'll have on your mind is how you could manage to take a bite out of somebody.

*(He flips more switches. A strobe light comes on, flickering across the stage, in addition to the other gadgets.)*

HARRY. You won't get away with it! Someone will report you! Etta...!

EINSTEIN. Oh, didn't I tell you? Even though your darling Etta won't be joining you at the altar, she is going to be a bride—the Bride of the Monster! *(He laughs maniacally. HARRY cries out and struggles savagely.)* I'm not sure if she'll be a blushing bride—that depends on whether or not I can figure out how to hook up the capillaries. The other attachments I've got down pat.

HARRY. You fiend!

EINSTEIN. *(Picking up the scalpel.)* I've been called worse. The creature called me terrible names until I convinced him he had better keep a civil tongue in his head. It belonged to a priest. *(Crossing above the table to behind HARRY's head. He grips HARRY's head with his free hand. HARRY struggles to no avail.)* Now, hold still! You don't want my hand to slip and cut your ear off!—you'd wind up looking like Van Gogh, the werewolf! *(He lowers the scalpel to the back of HARRY's neck. There is a BANGING of the door SL.)* Drat! Who is it!?!

PROFESSOR. *(Off SL.)* It's me—Professor Wonder.

EINSTEIN. Do you have the girl?

PROFESSOR. *(Voice.)* Uh...

ETTA. *(Off SL.)* Let go of me, Professor Wonder!

HARRY. Etta!

ETTA. *(Voice.)* Harry!

EINSTEIN. Wait a minute. *(He crosses to the door SL and turns the key to unlock it.)* It's open.

*(NICK flings the door open. PROFESSOR, ETTA and the troupe, except BARON, SURGE INTO THE ROOM, driving EINSTEIN SR.)*

NICK. Get out of the way, Einstein! We're wise to you!

EINSTEIN. What...!?!

PROFESSOR. Sorry, doc. They forced me to bring them here.

ETTA. *(Rushing to the gurney.)* Harry! He didn't...!?!

HARRY. No, darling, but you got here just in the nick of time! Untie me!

*(ETTA unties one wrist, HARRIET the other, DIANNE one ankle, TOOTIE the other. He will get off the gurney and push it out of the way in the UL corner. CLARA will cross above the table, pick up the beaker with her potion inside, and withdraw into her own thoughts. Meanwhile:)*

HARRIET. Giganticus, can you turn those machines off? The static electricity in the air is making my beard stand on end.

*(GIGAN moves around the room, flipping switches and turning dials. The strobe light and gadgets go off.)*

NICK. All right, doctor, I just want to know one thing!

EINSTEIN. What?

NICK. *(Rubbing his throat.)* Do you have any lozenges? My throat's been killing me!

PEARL & OPAL. *(Together.)* Nick!

NICK. Uh...right. Never mind.

DIANNE. The Professor told us everything, Harry—how Dr. Einstein planned to turn you into a monster, and then use Etta for spare parts on another one.

EINSTEIN. *(To PROFESSOR.)* Blabber-mouth!

HARRY. Dr. Einstein let some information slip, as well—he said the carnival has made lots of money, a fact the Professor kept hidden from you.

THE TROUPE EXCEPT CLARA. *(Together.)* What!?!

PROFESSOR. *(To EINSTEIN.)* Benedict Arnold!

TOOTIE. *(To PROFESSOR.)* All this time you've forced us to work for peanuts! If we were in Cairo, I'd have you thrown to the crocodiles!

PROFESSOR. Oh, shut up before I run over you with a vacuum cleaner.

*(PEARL and OPAL step in front of TOOTIE protectively.)*

PEARL. You'll have to go through us first!

OPAL. Right! Tootie's our friend!

TOOTIE. *(Putting her hands on their shoulders.)* Thank you, Opal, and Pearl, that was very brave of you.

PEARL. Was it? *(Beaming.)* It was, wasn't it?

HARRIET. No wonder you're in cahoots with Dr. Einstein, Professor —you're two of a kind: scoundrels!

GIGAN. *(Raising his fists.)* I'd knock your blocks off!...(*Lowering them.*)...but my lumbago has been acting up.

*(OLAF RUNS IN SL.)*

DOPPEL/OLAF. Mathter...! Mathter...! Der castle ith on vire! *(Noticing the others.)* Oh! Are you haffing a party?

EINSTEIN. No, you idiot!

DOPPEL/OLAF. You could haf fooled me.

EINSTEIN. Anyone could fool you, you half-wit!

ETTA. *(Angry; crossing to EINSTEIN.)* Leave him alone, Dr. Einstein! You have no right to be mean to Olaf! He might be dumber than a post, but he's a nicer person that you could ever hope to be!

DOPPEL/OLAF. That'th der nicest ting anyvon effer thed about me. I tink I'm goink to cry.

PROFESSOR. Hey! Didn't any of you jokers hear what he said!?! The castle is on fire! We have to get out of here!

EINSTEIN. An excellent suggestion, Professor. *(EINSTEIN grabs ETTA's arm and brings his other hand with the scalpel to her neck. ETTA and the others except CLARA gasp.)* I believe I'll take you up on it.

HARRY. Let her go!

*(He and the others, except PROFESSOR and CLARA, step toward ETTA and EINSTEIN.)*

EINSTEIN. *(Taking the scalpel closer.)* Stop! *(They stop in unison.)* Now, move aside!

*(They clear a path for him. Gripping ETTA, he pulls her toward the door SL.)*

ETTA. Take your hand off me!

EINSTEIN. Not until we're safely away from here, my dear. You're my insurance policy. *(He releases ETTA and takes the key from the lock. Gesturing with the scalpel.)* After you! You, too, Olaf! Fetch my money box from under my bed!

DOPPEL/OLAF. Yeth, mathter! *(He hurriedly EXITS and changes costumes for FREDRICK. ETTA steps out through the doorway. EINSTEIN puts the key in the lock on the outside.)* Don't bother trying to get out. This is a solid oak door—you'll never break it down.

HARRY. You can't lock us in here! We'll burn to death!

EINSTEIN. That's the idea. I prefer to leave no witnesses.

PROFESSOR. *(Crossing toward the door.)* Good plan.

EINSTEIN. I thought so.

*(He jabs the scalpel at PROFESSOR, making him jump back.)*

PROFESSOR. Hey!
EINSTEIN. Since your entire carnival troupe is going up in flames, our partnership is obviously at an end. And when I say "I'll leave no witnesses", I mean NO witnesses.

*(He slams and locks the door, EXITING with ETTA.)*

PROFESSOR. You louse!
HARRIET. That's funny—I had my mouth all worked up to say the same thing about you.
HARRY. Etta! She's a witness! That means Dr. Einstein plans to kill her, too, once he's got away from here! I've got to save her! *(He runs to the door and pulls on the knob frantically.)* Open the door! Somebody open the door!
BELLA. No one will hear you, Harry. The servants are sure to be fleeing for their lives. I'm afraid we're doomed!

*(The bat appears behind the window, flapping in place. If we see the fishing pole above the flat, that's okay—remember, the operative word for this play is "silly".)*

DIANNE. Is there nothing we can do?
BARON. *(Off UC with a high-pitched, thin bat-voice.)* The castle is on fire! The castle is on fire! Get out! Get out!

*(The others, except CLARA, turn toward the window.)*

TOOTIE. Baron! Thank goodness you're here! Dr. Einstein has locked us in! Fly in another window in the tower, transform into your human shape, and unlock the door!
BARON. *(Voice.)* You got it, Tootie!

*(The bat flaps off UL.)*

HARRY. What was that?

NICK. Our friend, Baron Biterondernek. He's a vampire.
HARRY. Oh, yeah, I heard about him—the fruit juice sipper.
HARRIET. That's our Baron.

*(BARON unlocks and opens the door SL. You might use a fog machine so that a low layer of smoke billows into the room when he enters.)*

BARON. You're free! *(Everyone except CLARA cheers.)* Get out quickly, everyone!

*(Everyone rushes out SL, EXITING. BELLA, noticing CLARA at the table, oblivious, runs to her, takes the beaker from her hand, puts it back onto the table, and grabs her hand.)*

BELLA. Come on, Madam Clara!

*(She pulls her SL.)*

CLARA. Ve're goink zomeplace else? Vhere?
BELLA. You're the psychic—guess!

*(They EXIT. PROFESSOR has lingered behind. When the others are gone, he crosses to the door SR, unbolts it, and opens it.)*

PROFESSOR. Hey! Ugly-puss!
MONSTER. *(Voice.)* Didn't make any noise...
PROFESSOR. Yeah, yeah... In case you're interested, the castle is on fire.

*(The MONSTER lets out a roar.)*

MONSTER. *(Voice.)* Fire! Fire burns! Scared of fire!
PROFESSOR. I thought you'd like to know your maker, Dr. Einstein, left you here to go up in flames. *(The MONSTER roars again, angry.)* What do you think about that?
MONSTER. *(Voice.)* Hate doctor! Want to hurt doctor!

PROFESSOR. I was hoping you'd say that. If you follow me, maybe we can catch up with him, and you can show him just how you feel.
MONSTER. *(Voice.)* Yes... Catch him! Hurt him!

*(PROFESSOR, pleased, runs to the door SL, stops, and turns back.)*

PROFESSOR. What are you waiting for!?!
MONSTER. *(Voice.)* Saying goodbye to mate... Goodbye, arm...goodbye leg...where did head go...?

*(With a disgusted look, PROFESSOR RUNS OUT SL. The lights go to a quick BLACKOUT. Frantic music fades in as the curtain closes. During the next scene, STAGEHANDS will strike the lab and arrange the study.)*

### Scene 5—The corridors. Immediately following.

*(The following scene should provide a tour de force for DOPPEL as he plays all the characters in it, making super-quick costume changes offstage as he delivers the dialog. The actor should be prepared to ad-lib extra dialog in character if he needs more time for the changes, though the quicker he can make them, the funnier the scene will be.)*
*(The music fades out as the lights fade up dimly on the forestage. No set pieces are used in this scene. Smoke from fog machines can be blown in from the wings and/or under the main curtain from behind.)*

DOPPEL/FREDRICK. *(RUSHING IN DL.)* Where is that girl!?! Heide! Cousin Heide! Where are you!?!

*(He EXITS DR and changes costumes for HEIDE.)*

DOPPEL/HEIDE. *(Voice.)* Vas zomevon callink mein name?
DOPPEL/FREDRICK. *(Voice.)* Yes. I was! You've got to go immediately!
DOPPEL/HEIDE. *(Voice.)* You mean I'm fired!?!

DOPPEL/FREDRICK. *(Voice.)* No, but you're going to be if you don't leave the castle at once!

DOPPEL/HEIDE. *(Voice.)* I don't understand...

DOPPEL/FREDRICK. *(Voice.)* Why does that not surprise me? Listen carefully, Heide... The...castle...is...on...fire. We have to leave.

DOPPEL/HEIDE. *(Voice.)* Der castle iss on vire!?! It vasn't me! I alvays unplug der iron fen I'fe finished vid der laundry!

DOPPEL/FREDRICK. *(Voice.)* I know it wasn't you—it was the villagers.

DOPPEL/HEIDE. *(Voice.)* Vhy vere der villagers doink our laundry?

DOPPEL/FREDRICK. *(Voice.)* They weren't, you silly girl! Oh, never mind... I need you to find Aunt Brunhilda and Great-grandmother Freida and tell them to flee.

DOPPEL/HEIDE. *(Voice.)* I can do dot.

DOPPEL/FREDRICK. *(Voice.)* Then go! Go!

DOPPEL/HEIDE. *(Voice.)* Ja! I go! *(HEIDE RUNS IN DR, carrying her feather duster, and hurries to DL.)* Goodness, gracious! Der castle's on vire! Der castle's on vire! *(She EXITS and changes costumes for BRUNHILDA.)* Aunt Brunhilda! Aunt Brunhilda!

DOPPEL/BRUNHILDA. *(Voice.)* What iss it, Heide? Vhy are you zo excited?

DOPPEL/HEIDE. *(Voice.)* Der castle iss on vire!...und I didn't do it!

DOPPEL/BRUNHILDA. *(Voice.)* Der castle iss on vire!?!

DOPPEL/HEIDE. *(Voice.)* Ja! *(Getting hysterical.)* Vhat are ve goink to do, Aunt Brunhilda!?! I don't vant to die! I don't vant to end up like a pig on der spit! Vhat are ve goink to do!?! *(There is a SMACK as if HEIDE was slapped.)* Ow... Vhat did you hit me for?

DOPPEL/BRUNHILDA. *(Voice.)* You ver gettink hysterical.

DOPPEL/HEIDE. *(Voice.)* I'd radder haf hysterics dan a dislocated jaw!

DOPPEL/BRUNHILDA. *(Voice.)* It did zee trick. Now, calmly head for der nearest exit.

DOPPEL/HEIDE. *(Voice.)* All right, Aunt Brunhilda. Oh! Oh!

DOPPEL/BRUNHILDA. *(Voice.)* Vhat iss it now?

DOPPEL/HEIDE. *(Voice.)* I joost remembered... Cousin Fredrick zed to tell both you und Great-grandmudder Freida to run for your lifes!

DOPPEL/BRUNHILDA. *(Voice.)* I'll find Auntie Freida. You go on.

DOPPEL/HEIDE. *(Voice.)* Oh. Okay... Zee you outzide.

DOPPEL/BRUNHILDA. *(RUNNING ON DL. She will hurry to DR, bosom flying all over the place.)* Dot Heide... She's a sveet child, but not der hottest burner on der stove. Auntie Freida! Auntie Freida!

*(She EXITS DR and changes costumes for FREIDA.)*

DOPPEL/FREIDA. *(Voice.)* Who iss?

DOPPEL/BRUNHILDA. *(Voice.)* Iss me, Auntie Freida—Brunhilda. I'fe been lookink effreevhere for you!

DOPPEL/FREIDA. *(Voice.)* Am I lost?

DOPPEL/BRUNHILDA. *(Voice.)* No, Auntie Freida.

DOPPEL/FREIDA. *(Voice.)* Oh, goot. Dus der doctor vish me to take zome tea to zomevon?

DOPPEL/BRUNHILDA. *(Voice.)* No, Auntie—your tea-toetink days are over. Der castle iss on vire!

DOPPEL/FREIDA. *(Voice. A cry, then:)* Der castle iss on vire!?! Haf you burned der beans again!?!

DOPPEL/BRUNHILDA. *(Voice.)* No, I didn't!...und dis is not anudder little kitchen vire—dis iss der real ting! Der whole kit-und-kerboodle! Ve haf to get out now!

DOPPEL/FREIDA. *(Voice.)* Get out...get out... Ja!

DOPPEL/BRUNHILDA. *(Voice.)* Go dot vay vhile I look for udder servants! Hurry!

DOPPEL/FREIDA. *(Voice.)* Ja! Ja! I hurry like der vind! *(FREIDA ENTERS DR. Her pumping arms and body language look like someone running like crazy, but her speed is the same as FREIDA's always is—super-slow. She gets to DC, stops, catches her breath, then continues in the same manner to DL.)* Like der vind...

*(She EXITS DL and changes costumes for OLAF. Dramatic music fades in as the lights fade out and plays a few beats.)*

### Scene 6—Dr. Einstein's study. Immediately following.

*(The music fades out as the lights fade up and the curtain opens. Fog machines can make smoke roll in at the archways and on the veranda which is still lit by moonlight. The moon still hangs against the backdrop. There are MOB SOUNDS from offstage, which can be recorded. After a beat, EINSTEIN RUSHES IN at the archway UR, dragging ETTA with him. He still carries the scalpel.)*

ETTA. Let me go!
EINSTEIN. Why? So you can run back to the tower and set your boy friend and the others free? No, my dear, you'll stay with me until we're well away from the castle.
ETTA. You're a mean, evil man!
EINSTEIN. That's your opinion. I see myself as a genius! Who else do you know who has built a man from scratch and given him life!?!
ETTA. That creature is not a man—it's a monster!
EINSTEIN. I'd like to see you do any better, Miss Smarty Pants! If you think he turned out ugly, you should have seen the parts I rejected! Enough chit-chat! I must see if the coast is clear. *(He opens the French doors and looks outside, cautiously.)* The mob is moving toward the front of the castle. In a moment, we'll be able to slip by them into the forest, unnoticed. I warn you—if you make a sound, it will be your last! Do you understand!?! *(ETTA doesn't answer.)* Well!?! Do you!?!
ETTA. *(Speaking with her lips clamped tightly together.)* You told me not to make a sound.
EINSTEIN. Where the villagers can hear you! Foolish girl! Do you understand you had better keep quiet!?!
ETTA. *(Speaking normally, but quietly.)* Yes, I understand.

*(OLAF RUSHES IN DL, dragging an old-fashioned looking chest which seems to be very heavy. Smoke might drift in with him.)*

DOPPEL/OLAF. Mathter! Mathter!
EINSTEIN. *(Crossing to CS, pulling ETTA.)* I'm right here, Olaf.

DOPPEL/OLAF. Tho I thee... I haf der money chest, mathter!
EINSTEIN. Tho I thee... I mean, I see! We're going to escape
through the woods. Stay close to me, Olaf.
DOPPEL/OLAF. Yeth, thur.

*(He steps right next to EINSTEIN. EINSTEIN and ETTA wrinkle their noses.)*

EINSTEIN. Not that close.

*(OLAF takes a step back.)*

ETTA. It's what you deserve for making him sleep in a pig sty.
EINSTEIN. Who asked you?

*(The others ad-lib excitedly off UR.)*

HARRY. *(Off UR.)* Etta! Etta, where are you!?!
EINSTEIN. Drat! Who freed them from the tower!?!

*(He smacks OLAF's hump.)*

DOPPEL/OLAF. Ow! It vasn't me, mathter!

*(HARRY and the troupe EXCEPT BARON and PROFESSOR RUSH IN UR. They will spread SR of the room.)*

HARRY. Etta! Thank goodness we found you!
ETTA. Oh, Harry...!

*(Unnoticed, the bat appears behind the French doors. It flies in place, looking in. The troupe starts ad-libbing together excitedly, comments like "Let her go", "We have to get out of here", etc.)*

EINSTEIN. Shut up! All you just...shut up!

*(He swings the scalpel in their direction. The troupe shuts up. PRO-*
*FESSOR RUNS IN UR.)*

DOPPEL/OLAF. You could haf thed, "Cut it out!". *(He makes a*
*snorty laugh at his own joke. EINSTEIN hits his hump.)* Ow! *(Muttering.)*
Zome people haf no thenth of humor...

EINSTEIN. *(Starts backing US toward the French doors, pulling*
*ETTA. OLAF edges with them.)* Come along, Etta. Say goodbye to Harry
for the last time.

*(The bat flies out of sight off UL of the door. HARRY and the troupe*
*cry out, ad-libbing for him to let her go. When EINSTEIN*
*reaches the open doorway, BARON STEPS IN behind the trio*
*from off UL.)*

BARON. You're not going anywhere, Dr. Einstein. *(EINSTEIN*
*wheels to face him.)*

EINSTEIN. Baron! Get out of our way, or I'll...

BARON. You'll what, doctor?

EINSTEIN. You asked for it! *(He appears to stab BARON with the*
*scalpel, actually thrusting it inches US of his chest. BARON smiles at*
*him.)* What...!?!

BARON. You forget, Dr. Einstein, you can't harm me with that—
I'm already dead. *(He grabs EINSTEIN around the throat with both*
*hands. EINSTEIN drops the scalpel and releases ETTA's arm, bring-*
*ing his hands up to BARON's wrists. ETTA stumbles to HARRY who*
*catches her. The troupe cheers.)* Now if you had come at me with a
stake, it would have been a different matter, of course.

EINSTEIN. *(Strangled.)* Olaf—get me a stake!

DOPPEL/OLAF. You vant rare, medium or vell done?

PROFESSOR. *(Rushing toward OLAF.)* While you're working it
out, let me give you a hand with that, Olaf.

HARRY. Oh, no, you don't!

*(He rushes toward PROFESSOR and grabs him. They begin to struggle.*
*The troupe and ETTA move US of them as HARRY and PROFESSOR*

*move to LC, forming a semi-circle above them. The troupe ad-libs en-couragement to HARRY. When it's clear Harry is getting the best of PROFESSOR:)*

PROFESSOR. Keep the money, just let me out of here!

*(He breaks free and RUNS OUT DL.)*

DOPPEL/OLAF. He'll be thorry... Vhen I came tru der hall, der ceiling vas about to give vay. *(There is a LOUD CRASH and PRO-FESSOR SCREAMS off DL.)* Thee vhat I mean?

EINSTEIN. *(Still struggling with BARON UR.)* Let-go-of-me!

*(He breaks BARON's grip on his throat and staggers backward to the arch-way UR. The MONSTER'S hand and arm appear from behind him; the hand grips his shoulder. This is, as before, all we'll see of MONSTER.)*

MONSTER. *(Voice, off UR.)* You bad! You leave me to burn!

*(The others turn to watch.)*

EINSTEIN. Believe it or not, I was planning to come right back and get you.

MONSTER. *(Voice.)* Not believe!

EINSTEIN. *(Muttering.)* I had to try. *(Out loud.)* Look, let's play your favorite game—hide and seek! You go hide in the tower and I'll cover my eyes and count to ten thousand. Then I'll come and look for you.

ETTA. You cad!

HARRY. He's trying to trick you...uh...Mr. Monster. He wants you to burn up with the castle.

EINSTEIN. Mind your own business!

BARON. The Professor was going to add you to our carnival troupe. We don't have much, but you're welcome to join us.

MONSTER. *(Voice.)* You nice—not like maker. Me belong here, not out in world. Let fire destroy me—and man who made me! You coming with me!

*(He pulls EINSTEIN toward the doorway.)*

EINSTEIN. What!?! Hold it!?! Bad idea! Heeeellllpppp...

*(He is pulled out of sight UR, EXITING with MONSTER.)*

ETTA. It looks like that's the end of Dr. Einstein.
HARRY. It serves him right. He should never have tried to tamper with nature.
DOPPEL/OLAF. Do you mean he'th gone for good?
ETTA. Yes, Olaf... And we will be, too, if we don't leave before the place goes up in flames.
BARON. This way, everyone!
DOPPEL/OLAF. Vait! What zhould I do vid dis?

*(Indicating the money box.)*

NICK. That's the money box?
DOPPEL/OLAF. Yeth, thur. It'th filled vid gold coins.
GIGAN. *(Crossing to OLAF.)* Let me give you a hand with it. *(He picks up the box and sets it on his shoulder. The others gasp.)* All I needed was the proper motivation. Now, let's get out of here!

*(Everyone rushes out through the French doors. OLAF trails after them.)*

DOPPEL/OLAF. By der vay... Are you acceptink job applications? I've alvays vanted to vork vid a carnival. I'm afraid I von't be able to get a recommendation from my last employer...

*(The lights fade out as the curtain closes. Soft music fades in. STAGEHANDS set the tree cutouts DR and DL. OLAF changes costumes for OTTO.)*

### Scene 7—A path in the forest. Shortly after.

*(The music fades out as the lights fade up on the forest, signifying moonlight. HARRY, ETTA and the troupe RUSH ON DL. GIGAN still carries the money box.)*

DIANNE. Does anyone know where we are?

NICK. I think our wagons are a little ways ahead.

HARRY. We're safe now. We can stop and catch our breath.

*(They stop DC, spreading out. Everyone catches his breath. CLARA will withdraw into her thoughts, ignoring the others.)*

ETTA. Where's Olaf?

PEARL. Oh, he went to his sty to gather his things.

OPAL. We told him he can come with us. Surely we can find Olaf something to do in the carnival.

NICK. What carnival? Now that the Professor is gone...

HARRIET. We can go on without him, Nick. You heard what Harry said in the tower—we've been making lots of money all along. We just didn't know it. Right, Harry?

HARRY. That's what Dr. Einstein said.

BELLA. I bet if we give Professor Wonder's wagon a thorough search, there's no telling how much loot we'll find hidden away.

GIGAN. The last thing the Professor said was, "Keep the money". I figure that makes it ours. *(He sets the money box on the ground.)* That should include what's in here, too, since he was giving Dr. Einstein the profit that should have gone to us.

*(He opens the lid. Big reaction from everyone as GIGAN reaches in and pulls out a handful of gold coins which he lets trickle through his fingers back into the chest.)*

DIANNE. We're rich! I'm going to get tattooed from head to toe!

TOOTIE. Ramses, here I come!

PEARL & OPAL. *(Together, to each other.)* Our own bedrooms!

HARRY. I guess that means you can all retire now.

ETTA. If you want to, that is...

BARON. Actually, I think I'm too young to retire; I'm only two hundred.

HARRIET. I'd kind of miss the travel...

PEARL. But most of all...

OPAL. ...we'd miss you guys.

*(The others ad-lib agreement.)*

TOOTIE. What the heck! Retirement can wait! Let's keep the carnival together!

*(The others ad-lib agreement enthusiastically. OTTO ENTERS DL.)*

DOPPEL/OTTO. Dere you are! I'm glad to zee you got avay from der castle before it burned to der ground.
ETTA. Otto!
HARRY. You weren't part of the mob?
DOPPEL/OTTO. No. Vhen mein nephew, Gregor, tolt me vhat our relatives vere goink to do, I tolt him I had a cold und couldn't come vid him. Den I hooked up mein horse, Rudolph, to der carnival vagons and pulled dem out of der mud. You should all go now, qvickly!
DIANNE. How sweet...
BELLA. How can we thank you?

*(The troupe ad-libs their thanks.)*

DOPPEL/OTTO. You're velcome. I figure dot Dr. Einstein vas an efil man who had you fooled, joost as vee vere, at first. Mein dumkoff relations might not zee it dot vay, zo you had better leaf vhile you can. You two kids I brought from der station...*(He takes a good look at HARRY.)*...my goodness, your beard and hair zertainly grow fast!...if you vill come vid me, I'll take you back. Dere's a train leafing for Lipsync in a few minutes.
ETTA. How wonderful! Come, Harry, let us depart at once!
HARRY. *(Taking her hands in his.)* You go, Etta—I cannot.
ETTA. What? But, Harry...
HARRY. You must go back to the university without me, complete your studies, and make a happy life for yourself. It must be a life I cannot be a part of.
ETTA. Harry...

HARRY. Don't you see we have to go our separate ways? I will ask our new friends if I can join their carnival. With them is where I belong, dearest, since I—like them—am a freak. *(To THE troupe.)* No offense intended. *(The troupe's expressions show they accept his apology, but grudgingly. To ETTA:)* Go...
DOPPEL/OTTO. *(Gesturing her to join him.)* Hurry...hurry...

*(Doing a very corny bit, ETTA slowly steps back from HARRY, their arms extending until only their fingertips touch, then they break. She turns and crosses to OTTO, crying. They start to exit, but stop when:)*

CLARA. *(Coming out of her reverie.)* Der potion zhould haf vorked! *(The troupe mutters "Yeah, sure", etc.)* Vell, it zhould! I had all der ingredients right here in mein pockets! *(She thrusts her hands into her pockets, looks puzzled, then brings out a quarter-size piece of raw spinach leaf.)* Vas is dis? Ah! Der leaf from der volfbane plant! I accidentally left out der volfbane leaf! Dot's der most important ting! No vonder der potion vas a flop! Eat dis, Harry! Der udder ingredients are already in your system—eat dis und der curse vill be lifted!

*(She thrusts the leaf at him.)*

ETTA. *(To OTTO, in answer to his puzzled look.)* Harry's a werewolf.
DOPPEL/OTTO. Oh, okay... Dot explains der fuzzy face.
CLARA. Eat it!
HARRY. *(To ETTA.)* Should I...?
ETTA. Yes! Yes, dearest! If there's any hope at all...

*(The troupe looks very dubious. HARRY puts the leaf into his mouth and chews it. Suddenly, he looks stricken. All react, gasp. OTTO puts a protective arm around ETTA; she clings to his other hand with both of hers and watches HARRY, frightened. HARRY grabs his throat, choking. The troupe makes a semi-circle below HARRY, hiding him from the audience, ETTA and OTTO. HARRY removes the wig and beard and hands it to a STAGEHAND behind the curtain at its split. The troupe ad-libs astonishment, then parts to reveal HARRY.)*

HARRY. *(Dazed.)* Food! I want...turnip greens! Lima beans! Squash! *(Everyone cheers. He shakes his head, clearing it.)* Madam Clara! The potion worked! I'm cured!

*(Bigger cheer from all. ETTA rushes into his arms.)*

ETTA. Oh, darling! *(They kiss.)* Madam Clara, you're marvelous!
CLARA. It vas nuzzink.
HARRY. Oh, yes, it was!

*(He kisses CLARA on one cheek as ETTA kisses her on the other.)*

PEARL. We're really proud of you, Madam Clara!
OPAL. We'll never doubt you again!

*(The troupe ad-libs their support enthusiastically.)*

DOPPEL/OTTO. *(Wiping away a tear.)* I joost luff happy endings. Come, or ve'll miss der train! Der rest of you—off! Off!

*(The troupe starts DR. GIGAN and NICK carry the chest between them. All fawn over CLARA.)*

BARON. I have a suggestion—let's paint over Professor Wonder's name on our wagons and put a new one in its place: Madam Clara's Amazing Carnival!

*(The other agree.)*

NICK. Uh...Madam Clara, do you think you could mix up a potion for my sore throat...?
BELLA. I could use something to cut down my appetite...
GIGAN. I'll need a liniment after all this lifting...
CLARA. All right! All right! I'll get to all of you! *(She stops DR and holds up her hands to stop the others. To HARRY and ETTA:)* Ve vill be playink in Lipsync in zix veeks.
HARRY. We'll see you then!

*(ETTA blows them a kiss. The troupe EXITS DR, waving to HARRY and ETTA who wave back.)*

DOPPEL/OTTO. Dis vay...dis vay...

*(He EXITS DL. HARRY and ETTA join hands and cross to DL.)*

ETTA. You know, Harry, in spite of all we've been through with the doctor and Professor Wonder and that horrible, but pitiful, monster, I'm still glad we came to Castle Einstein. We made some nice, new friends, and Madam Clara was able to cure you.

HARRY. You're right, Etta, as usual. Now we can be married for—thanks to her—I no longer have the werewolf's curse!

*(They EXIT DL, but HARRY's leg reappears immediately, aimed at a tree just US of the exit.)*

ETTA. *(Off DL.)* Harry!

*(The leg zips quickly out of sight as, we assume, ETTA pulls HARRY away.)*

**BLACKOUT**

*(Lively music comes in. The curtain will open on the study where the cast takes their bows.)*

**CURTAIN**

## PRODUCTION NOTES

### STYLE

"Werewolf's Curse" is a spoof of Universal Studio's classic horror films of the 1930's, "The Wolf Man", "Frankenstein", and "Dracula" in particular. The style of acting in these movies is very different from today's more naturalistic approach. The cast should watch any or all of these films and note how the actors speak with such precise articulation that even the American characters sound faintly British, and that the dialog, more flowery than "real" speech, is delivered with somewhat heightened intensity, even in an "everyday" conversation. Your actors who will be using Teutonic accents should pay special attention to the accents of the villagers in these movies. Also, note the actors' gestures and body language; in these classics, the acting hasn't progressed all that far from the silent movie style. In short, camp it up and have fun!

### TEMPO

As you've no doubt noted, the play is structured so that short scenes in front of the main curtain alternate with scenes set in the main set (the study) and the insert set (the lab). Jumping back and forth for 16 scenes adds to the feel of a movie in which various locations are used, even though in the play the locations on the forestage are mostly suggested. Your tech crew should set and strike the scenery as quickly as possible so that the tempo of the play never lags. Using music between scenes will help the play to flow smoothly and briskly.

## DOPPEL'S COSTUME CHANGES

Doppel will certainly be the hardest working member of your cast—at least physically. Part of the fun in watching him switch among the seven characters he plays comes from seeing him exit, only to reappear very quickly as someone else—especially in Act II, Scene 5. To achieve these quick changes, Doppel will have to have dressers help him. I would suggest two for the costumes (one to take them off, one to put the next one on) and one for wigs and makeup. In Act II, Scene 5 it would be good to have at least two dressers off DL and two off DR, if not more. Doppel might be able to facilitate some changes by underdressing at times, such as wearing Freida's dress, for example, over another costume. Constructing the costumes with Velcro rather than zippers would probably help the rapid changes as well.

## PROPERTY PLOT

### PRE-SET:

All of the items used on the lab table can be pre-set from the beginning.
They are:

Lab equipment
Electronic gadgets (optional)
Pencil & journal
Syringe
Small bottle of colored water
Beaker of colored water
Vial of water with pearl onion inside
Candle or sterno under beaker
Matches
Scalpel (dulled)
Plate/chicken legs covered with napkin (behind other objects)
Also pre-set in lab:
Whip on hook
"Body" under sheet on gurney
Key in lock of door SL
Fake beard & wig behind screen

### During Act I, Scene 3:

Strike coffee items from coffee table

### Between Act I, Scenes 4 & 5:

Place painting on stand in place

### Between Act I, Scenes 5 & 6:

Strike painting on stand

### During Act I, Scene 8:

Strike fake hand from lab table
Strike tea cup/saucer from study table

### During Act I, Scene 9:

Pull full moon cutout into view

### Between Acts:

Place wall bracket on stand in place
Add moon cutout to study backdrop
Add bowl of fruit including punctured orange to study table

### Between Act II, Scenes 1 & 2:

Strike wall bracket on stand

### During Act II, Scene 2:

Fly rubber bat

### During Act II, Scene 3:

Tie Harry to gurney with rope

## During Act II, Scene 4:

Fly rubber bat

## During Act II, Scene 6:

Fly rubber bat

## PERSONAL PROPS:

Suitcase—Harry
Suitcase—Etta
Handkerchief—Etta
Tray w/coffee pot & coffee, 3 cups, 3 saucers, creamer & sugar bowl, 3 spoons—Freida
Wire rim glasses—Freida
Pencil/paper—Einstein
Scabbard/sword—Nick
Umbrella—Tootie
Fake hand—Monster
Handkerchief—Harry
Feather duster—Heide
Burlap bag w/mannequin parts—Olaf
Cup of tea on saucer—Brunhilda
Potion ingredients/Alka-Seltzer—Clara
Holster & gun (not used)—Hans
Axes, pitchforks, torches—Mob
Money box—Olaf

## COSTUME PLOT

HARRY PATE—30's style suit, tie, shoes, fedora hat, coat (Act I, Scenes 1 & 2); slacks and sport shirt (Act I, Scene 5 till end of play)

ETTA GREENLEAF—30's style dress, shoes, coat, cloche hat (Act I, Scenes 1 & 2); different dress or skirt and blouse (Act I, Scene 5 till end of play)

DR. EINSTEIN—dark slacks, dark shoes, white shirt, white lab coat

PROFESSOR WONDER—loud print suit, shoes, shirt, bow tie; for Act I, Scene 3 a straw boater hat

BARON BITERONDERNEK—tuxedo, dress shirt, formal bow tie, black dress shoes, black cape with red lining

HARRIET—Everyday 30's style dress, shoes; for Act I, Scene 3 a coat

DIANNE NEEDLES—carnival costume: one-piece bathing suit, heels; for Act I, Scene 3 a cloak

GIGANTICUS—carnival costume: leotard, tights, leopard-skin tunic, boots

OPAL & PEARL JOINER—Everyday 30's style dresses, shoes; for Act I, Scene 3 coats and hats

NICK GILLETTE—black slacks, colorful shirt with sleeves that blouse at the wrist, sash for belt, boots, bolero jacket, sword in scabbard

MADAM CLARA VOYANT—gypsy outfit: peasant blouse and skirt, beads, bracelets, ankle-high boots, scarf on head; for Act I, Scene 3 a shawl

BELLA—carnival costume: harem girl outfit, shoes that curl up on the ends, if possible; for Act I, Scene 3 a large veil

TOOTIEFRUITTEE—bandages, 30's style evening gown, heels, wig, tiara; for Act I, Scene 3 a cape and umbrella

OTTO—farmer's work pants, shirt, boots, battered hat

FREDRICK—tuxedo, dress shirt, formal tie, dress shoes

FREIDA—long black dress, black stockings, black old-lady shoes, white wig

OLAF—Dutch boy wig, dirty old clothes and boots, hump on back

HEIDE—dirndl, white leggings, Mary Jane shoes, blonde wig with pigtails

BRUNHILDA—peasant blouse and skirt, white leggings, flat shoes, wig with coiled braids

HANS—constable's uniform, helmet, boots, holster with gun

MOB—Items to throw over the cast's costumes: old, worn coats, capes shawls, scarves, mufflers, blankets, etc.

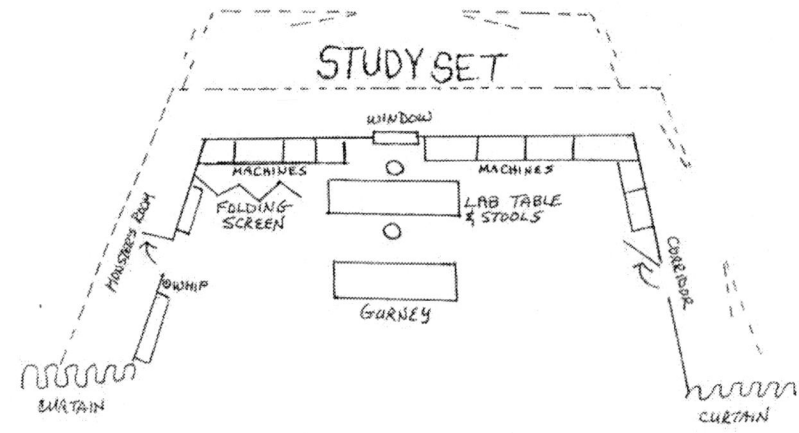

STUDY SET

WINDOW

MACHINES          MACHINES

FOLDING
SCREEN                    LAB TABLE
                         & STOOLS

MONSTER'S ROOM

WHIP                          CORRIDOR

GURNEY

CURTAIN                                   CURTAIN

Dr. Einstein's Laboratory

FOREST BACKDROP

BALUSTRADE
VERANDA

BACKING                  BACKING

TO LABORATORY     ARCHWAY     FRENCH DOORS     ARCHWAY     TO GUEST ROOMS
PLATFORM

GLOBE             TABLE      BACKING

BOOKCASES

DESK & CHAIRS          CHAIR          HALLWAY

DOUBLE DOORS

BELL PULL

TABLE & CHAIRS        COFFEE TABLE     SOFA

Dr. Einstein's Study

# Also By
# Billy St. John

The Abduction

The Disappearance Of The Three Little Pigs

Here Comes The Bride...
And There Goes The Groom

Herr Kutter, The Barbaric Barber

Is There A Comic In The House?

The Plot, Like Gravy, Thickens

The Reunion

Senior Follies

The Werewolf's Curse

You Could Die Laughing

Please visit our website **samuelfrench.com** for complete
descriptions and licensing information

## MURDER AT CAFÉ NOIR
David Landau
Music and Lyrics by Nikki Stern

*Mystery / 4m, 3f / Interior*

The most popular mystery dinner show in the country, *Murder at Café Noir* has enjoyed weekly productions coast to coast since its premiere in 1989. This forties detective story come to life features Rick Archer, P.I., out to find a curvaceous runaway on the forgotten island of Mustique, a place stuck in a black and white era. The owner of the Café Noir has washed ashore, murdered, and Rick's quarry was the last person seen with him. He employs his hard boiled talents to find the killer. Was it the French madame and club manager, the voodoo priestess, the shyster British attorney, the black marketeer or the femme fatale? The audience votes twice on what they want Rick to do next and these decisions change the flow of this comic tribute to the Bogart era.

"Fast and funny satire."
– *Los Angeles Times*

This whodunit is darn good it's the kind of show that lingers on you mind, like a dame's perfume
– *Maryland Journal*

# SAMUEL FRENCH STAFF

**Nate Collins**
President

**Ken Dingledine**
Director of Operations,
Vice President

**Bruce Lazarus**
Executive Director,
General Counsel

**Rita Maté**
Director of Finance

ACCOUNTING

**Lori Thimsen** | Director of Licensing Compliance
**Nehal Kumar** | Senior Accounting Associate
**Glenn Halcomb** | Royalty Administration
**Jessica Zheng** | Accounts Receivable
**Andy Lian** | Accounts Payable
**Charlie Sou** | Accounting Associate
**Joann Mannello** | Orders Administrator

BUSINESS AFFAIRS

**Caitlin Bartow** | Assistant to the Executive Director

CORPORATE COMMUNICATIONS

**Abbie Van Nostrand** | Director of Corporate
Communications

CUSTOMER SERVICE AND LICENSING

**Brad Lohrenz** | Director of Licensing Development
**Laura Lindson** | Licensing Services Manager
**Kim Rogers** | Theatrical Specialist
**Matthew Akers** | Theatrical Specialist
**Ashley Byrne** | Theatrical Specialist
**Jennifer Carter** | Theatrical Specialist
**Annette Storckman** | Theatrical Specialist
**Dyan Flores** | Theatrical Specialist
**Sarah Weber** | Theatrical Specialist
**Nicholas Dawson** | Theatrical Specialist
**David Kimple** | Theatrical Specialist

EDITORIAL

**Amy Rose Marsh** | Literary Manager
**Ben Coleman** | Literary Associate

MARKETING

**Ryan Pointer** | Marketing Manager
**Courtney Kochuba** | Marketing Associate
**Chris Kam** | Marketing Associate

PUBLICATIONS AND PRODUCT DEVELOPMENT

**Joe Ferreira** | Product Development Manager
**David Geer** | Publications Manager
**Charlyn Brea** | Publications Associate
**Tyler Mullen** | Publications Associate
**Derek P. Hassler** | Musical Products Coordinator
**Zachary Orts** | Musical Materials Coordinator

OPERATIONS

**Casey McLain** | Operations Supervisor
**Elizabeth Minski** | Office Coordinator, Reception
**Coryn Carson** | Office Coordinator, Reception

SAMUEL FRENCH BOOKSHOP (LOS ANGELES)

**Joyce Mehess** | Bookstore Manager
**Cory DeLair** | Bookstore Buyer
**Sonya Wallace** | Bookstore Associate
**Tim Coultas** | Bookstore Associate
**Alfred Contreras** | Shipping & Receiving

LONDON OFFICE

**Anne-Marie Ashman** | Accounts Assistant
**Felicity Barks** | Rights & Contracts Associate
**Steve Blacker** | Bookshop Associate
**David Bray** | Customer Services Associate
**Robert Cooke** | Assistant Buyer
**Stephanie Dawson** | Amateur Licensing Associate
**Simon Ellison** | Retail Sales Manager
**Robert Hamilton** | Amateur Licensing Associate
**Peter Langdon** | Marketing Manager
**Louise Mappley** | Amateur Licensing Associate
**James Nicolau** | Despatch Associate
**Martin Phillips** | Librarian
**Panos Panayi** | Company Accountant
**Zubayed Rahman** | Despatch Associate
**Steve Sanderson** | Royalty Administration Supervisor
**Douglas Schatz** | Acting Executive Director
**Roger Sheppard** | I.T. Manager
**Debbie Simmons** | Licensing Sales Team Leader
**Peter Smith** | Amateur Licensing Associate
**Garry Spratley** | Customer Service Manager
**David Webster** | UK Operations Director
**Sarah Wolf** | Rights Director